Also by Michael Bond:

Monsieur Pamplemousse Mysteries
*Published by Fawcett Books:*

MONSIEUR PAMPLEMOUSSE

MONSIEUR PAMPLEMOUSSE AND THE SECRET
MISSION

*Books for Children*

The Paddington Bear books

# MONSIEUR PAMPLEMOUSSE ON THE SPOT

## A GASTRONOMIC MYSTERY

# Michael Bond

FAWCETT CREST • NEW YORK

A Fawcett Crest Book
Published by Ballantine Books
Copyright © 1986 by Michael Bond

Library of Congress Catalog Card Number: 86-22206

ISBN 0-449-21338-2

This edition published by arrangement with Beaufort Books, Inc.

No character in this book is intended to represent any actual person; all the incidents of the story are entirely fictional in nature.

Manufactured in the United States of America

First Ballantine Books Edition: May 1988

# CONTENTS

1 'OPERATION SOUFFLÉ'     1
2 STRANGER IN THE NIGHT     23
3 A CAUSE FOR CELEBRATION     46
4 TAKING THE WATERS     65
5 L'INSTITUT DES BEAUX ARBRES     87
6 POMMES FRITES MAKES A DISCOVERY     112
7 THE PICNIC     136
8 A MEAL TO END ALL MEALS     156
9 APÉRITIFS WITH MADAME GRANTE     180

# 1

## 'OPERATION SOUFFLÉ'

'*PARDON, MONSIEUR.*'

Monsieur Pamplemousse jumped as a figure in evening dress suddenly materialised at his right elbow. Hastily sliding a large paperback edition of the collected works of Sir Arthur Conan Doyle beneath the folds of a snow-white tablecloth draped over his lap, he pulled himself together and in a split second made the mental leap from the austerity of number 221B Baker Street, London, Angleterre, to the unquestionably less than harsh reality of his opulent surroundings in the dining-room of Les Cinq Parfaits, Haute Savoie, France.

Inclining his head to acknowledge but not necessarily welcome the waiter's presence, he diverted his attention with some reluctance from the adventures of Sherlock Holmes to focus on a single cream-coloured card listing the various delights of the *menu gas-tronomique*. He was all too aware as he scanned the menu that his every movement was being followed by a third pair of eyes on the other side of a large picture-window to his right and he shifted his chair in an anti-clockwise direction to avoid their unblinking gaze.

Almost immediately, following a barely perceptible signal from the maître d'hôtel, a bevy of under-waiters descended on his table, rearranged the cutlery symmetrically in front of him, rotated the plate so that the Parfait motif was in line, adjusted the vase of flowers slightly, and then drew a dark-green velvet curtain a few inches to its left, blotting out as they did so part of Lac Léman, the misty foothills of the mountains beyond, and an unseemly intruder in the foreground.

Almost as quickly as it had arrived the entourage again melted discreetly into the background, but not before a large, wet, freshly vaselined nose reappeared on the other side of the window and pressed itself firmly against a fresh area of glass.

Monsieur Pamplemousse gave a sigh. Pommes Frites was being more than a little difficult that evening. He shuddered to think what the outside of the window would be like when it caught the rays of the morning sun.

'Pardon, *Monsieur*.' The maître d'hôtel leaned across. 'May I point out a slight change in the menu? The *Soufflé Surprise* is off.'

'The *Soufflé Surprise* is off?' Monsieur Pamplemousse repeated the words slowly, as if he could hardly believe his ears. 'But that is not possible.'

To say that he had ploughed his way through six or

seven previous courses with but one end in view, that of tasting the creation for which, above all, Les Cinq Parfaits was famous, would have been a gross misstatement of the facts; an unforgivable calumny. Every course had been sheer perfection; not just a plateau, but one of a series of individual peaks, each a thing of beauty in its own right, offering both satisfaction and a tantalising foretaste of other delights to come. If he stopped right where he was he could hardly complain. It had been a memorable meal. All the same, to take the mountaineering analogy still further, there was only one Everest. To have travelled so far and yet not to have scaled the highest point of all, that which was embodied in the *Soufflé Surprise*, would be a great disappointment.

He was tempted to ask why, if it was off, was he being shown the menu where the two words *Soufflé* and *Surprise* were printed very clearly between *fromage* and *café*. It was rubbing salt into the wound.

He glanced around the crowded restaurant. 'There will be many sorrowful faces in Les Cinq Parfaits tonight.'

'*Oui, Monsieur.*' The waiter clearly shared his unhappiness.

'What have you instead?'

Looking, if possible, even more ill at ease, the waiter waved towards a large trolley heading in their direction.

'We have our collection of home-made sorbets. *Monsieur* may have a *panaché*—a selection if he so wishes.'

'But I have already eaten a sorbet,' said Monsieur Pamplemousse testily. 'I had one between the *Omble* and the *Quenelles de veau*.'

And very nice it had been too—a *Granité au vin de*

3

*Saint Emilion*, made with something rather better than a *vin ordinaire* if he was any judge, a *Grand Cru Classé* to which orange and lemon had been added, the whole garnished with a fresh, white peach inlaid with mint leaves. A palate-cleanser of the very first order. He had awarded it full marks on the pad concealed beneath a fold in his right trouser leg.

'*Fruits de saison*? We have wild *framboises* ... gathered on the mountainside just before nightfall by girls from the village. They are still warm from their aprons . . .'

'*Fruits de saison*?' Without raising his voice Monsieur Pamplemousse managed to imbue the words with exactly the right amount of scorn.

'A *crème caramel, Monsieur*?' There was the barest hint of desperation in the waiter's voice. 'Made with eggs from our own chickens, fed from the day they were born on nothing but . . .'

'A *crème caramel*?' Aware that he was beginning to sound like an ageing actor milking every line which came his way, Monsieur Pamplemousse decided to try another tack. 'Have you nothing which includes the word *pâtisserie*?'

Even as he posed the question he knew what the answer would be. It explained the absence of many of the customary tit-bits earlier in the meal. An absence which he had noted with a certain amount of relief at the time, fearing the outcome of any battle involving mind over matter.

The waiter leaned over his table in order to remove an imaginary bread crumb. 'I regret, *Monsieur*, the *pâtisserie* is not of a standard this evening that we in Les Cinq Parfaits would feel able to serve to our customers.' He lowered his voice still further. 'As for the *Soufflé Surprise* . . . pouf!' A low whistling sound somehow reminiscent of a hot-air balloon collapsing ignominiously escaped his lips. He looked for a moment as if he were about to say something else and then decided against it, aware that he might already have spoken out of turn and betrayed a position of trust.

Monsieur Pamplemousse decided not to press the man any further. Ordering the *framboises* he sat back in order to consider the matter. Clearly all was not well in the kitchens of Les Cinq Parfaits, and if all was not well then it put him in something of a quandary.

His presence there was only semi-official, a kind of treat on the part of his employers, the publishers of *Le Guide*. It had been arranged by a grateful Director following the success of a mission on his behalf in the Loire valley. Nevertheless, implicit in the visit was an appraisal of the restaurant, an extra opinion concerning a matter which had been exercising the minds of his superiors for some considerable time. Work was never far away when food was on the table.

Just as *Le Guide* was by general consent the doyen of the French gastronomic guides, so Les Cinq Parfaits was considered the greatest of all French restaurants, which in most people's eyes meant the best in all the world.

Set like a jewel in the hills east of Evian and overlooking the lake, its walls were lined with photographs of the high and mighty, the rich and famous, who in their time had made the pilgrimage to its ever open doors. Presidents came and went, royalty rose and fell, but Les Cinq Parfaits seemed set to remain where it was for ever.

5

In an area devoted to those whose waistlines were sadly in need of reduction, or were beyond redemption, where consequently cuisine was, generally speaking, *basse* rather than *haute*, Les Cinq Parfaits had proved the exception to the rule and had thrived.

For many years possessor of three stars in Michelin, maximum toques in Gault Millau, and one of less than a dozen restaurants in France to enjoy the supreme accolade of three Stock Pots in *Le Guide*, it was an open secret that it was only a matter of time before one of the three rival guides broke ranks and awarded Les Cinq Parfaits an extra distinction of some kind.

Therein lay the rub. Such a break with tradition, were it to backfire, would lay whoever was responsible open to all manner of criticism. On the other hand, to delay, to be second, would be to risk the accusation of being a follower rather than a leader. It was a knotty problem and no mistake.

If three Stock Pots represented perfection, then a fourth would need to stand for something even more absolute. On the showing that evening, one of the cinq Parfaits, either Monsieur Albert, the father, or one of his four sons, Alain, Edouard, Gilbert or Jean-Claude, was failing to live up to the family name.

Monsieur Pamplemousse glanced around the room. Like all restaurants of its class, staff seemed to outnumber the diners. His notes and reference cards upstairs would give him the exact answer, but he judged the capacity to be about sixty *couverts*. All the tables were full, many of them would have been booked weeks if not months ahead; the clientèle was international. Waiters switched from speaking French to German to English and back again with practised ease.

The ceremony of the lifting of the silver salvers was in full swing. No dish arrived in the dining-room uncovered. No matter how many guests were seated round a table, for the waiter to ask who had ordered what was regarded as a cardinal sin, and the lifting of all the covers in unison was a theatrical gesture which never failed to draw the gastronomical equivalent of a round of applause.

At the next table a waiter who had just finished translating the entire menu into perfect German was now performing the same feat in English for another family. From the snatches of conversation he'd overheard when they arrived he gathered the daughter was at a local finishing school. Clearly her parents were not getting value for money.

Beyond them, at a smaller table, a young girl was sitting alone. From her blonde hair and the colour of her skin, and the fact that she seemed to be on nodding terms with the family at the next table, he guessed she must be English too. Probably at the same finishing school as their daughter. She couldn't have been more than eighteen or nineteen.

He wondered what she was doing there. She seemed oddly out of place and ill at ease, rather as if she was waiting for someone who she knew was going to let her down. Irrationally he found himself wanting to go across and ask if he could help in any way, but he resisted for fear his action might be misinterpreted, as it certainly would be by the other diners, if not by the girl herself. People always thought the worst. Once or twice she looked up quickly and caught him watching her, then just as quickly she looked down again, colouring in a becoming manner.

Holmes would have known all about her by now. He would have built up a complete picture in his mind, picking up some detail to do with the way she wore her belt or the cut and style of her dress.

'Borrowed for the evening, my dear Watson. And in a hurry too. You can tell by the way it doesn't quite match her nail-varnish.'

With difficulty he disengaged himself from the scene in order to return to his book. Reading it was really a labour of love; a holiday task he had set himself—a chance to improve his English while at the same time meeting up again with one of his favourite characters.

The stories were as unlike his own experiences in the Paris Sûreté as it was possible to imagine, and yet there was a certain fascination about them that he found irresistible. The particular story he was reading— *The Hound of the Baskervilles*—was a case in point. He had barely reached the second page when Holmes, from a brief examination of a man's walking-stick, had deduced that the owner was a country doctor who had trained at a large London hospital, left when he was little more than a senior student, was still under thirty years of age, amiable, absent-minded, and the possessor of a favourite dog, larger than a terrier and smaller than a mastiff.

Rereading the passage reminded Monsieur Pamplemousse of Pommes Frites. He looked round, but the face was no longer pressed against the window. It didn't need the intellectual powers of a Sherlock Holmes to tell him that his own particular Watson had gone off in a huff, and even though Pommes

Frites' exclusion from the meal had not been of his choosing he felt a sudden pricking of his conscience.

The discovery when they arrived at Les Cinq Parfaits that dogs were *interdits* had been a bitter disappointment. The ban had been imposed after a visiting captain of industry had been set upon one evening by a Dobermann Pinscher belonging to a disgruntled shareholder. It was understandable up to a point, but it was like forbidding visitors to the Eiffel Tower because someone had once been caught trying to place a bomb underneath it; hard to accept and impossible to explain to a creature whose powers of reasoning didn't follow such convoluted paths.

Not that the four-legged visitors to Les Cinq Parfaits did badly for themselves. The kennel area behind the main building was a model of its kind, the service was impeccable, with staffing levels scarcely less than in the restaurant itself. The straw was changed twice daily and there was a choice of food which was served from china plates bearing the hotel crest. Had there been paw-operated bell-pushes Monsieur Pamplemousse wouldn't have been surprised. At fifty francs a day, full pension, *service compris*, it was incredibly good value.

All the same, it wasn't like sharing a table, and in the event Pommes Frites had taken the whole thing rather badly, just as Monsieur Pamplemousse had feared.

Pommes Frites had a simplistic approach to life. Black, to him, was black. White was white. The shortest distance between two points was a straight line, and restaurants were for eating in, regardless of race, colour or breed. Rules of entry which showed any form of discrimination were beyond his comprehension.

Equally, Monsieur Pamplemousse had to admit that he missed Pommes Frites' company. Not just the occasional warmth of a head resting on his shoe, or the nuzzling up of a body against his leg, but also his views on the food, often conveyed by the raising of an eyebrow or a discreet wag of his tail.

Pommes Frites had a bloodhound's sensitivity to smells and to taste, a sensitivity sharpened by his early training with the Paris police and honed finer still during travels with his master over the length and breadth of France. Had they but known it, there were many restaurants who owed their placing in *Le Guide* to Pommes Frites' taste-buds, and Monsieur Pamplemousse would have given a great deal to have noted down his reaction to the meal he had just eaten.

He gazed out of the window at the lights of Lausanne, twinkling on the Swiss side of the lake. Somewhere in-between a steamer slowly made its way back to Geneva. He looked at his watch. It was still barely ten o'clock. He had dined early. There would be time for a stroll before retiring to bed. Perhaps he could take Pommes Frites for an extra long walk that night to help make up for things. There were some emergency biscuits in the boot of the car. When they got back he would open the packet as a special treat.

He glanced up again as a waiter came towards him carrying a silver tray bearing not, as he might have expected, a dish containing a mound of wild raspberries, but a plate on which reposed a single light-blue envelope. He frowned, recognising the colour of the hotel stationery. Who could possibly be sending him a note?

As the waiter disappeared again he picked up a

knife and slit open the envelope, aware that the party at the next table was watching him curiously. Inside there was a sheet of white telex paper and underneath a duplicate in pink. The message was short and to the point; a single word in fact. The word was ESTRAGON.

To say that Monsieur Pamplemousse blanched visibly as he digested it would have been to cast aspersions both on his ability to conceal his true feelings and on the subdued and subtle lighting conceived by the architect responsible for the interior design of the restaurant. Bearing in mind the sometimes astronomical size of the bills, blanching of any kind was filtered out by rays which purposely emanated from the warmer end of the spectrum.

Nevertheless, he felt a quickening of his pulse as he carefully refolded the message and slipped it between the pages of his book to mark where he left off. Any further reading was out of the question. Had he been Sherlock Holmes he would probably have reached for his violin in the hope of applying the panacea of music to soothe his racing thoughts. Instead, Monsieur Pamplemousse did the next best thing; he picked up a spoon and fork. More waiters were heading in his direction. It would be a pity to let the efforts of all those village girls with their bulging aprons go to waste.

The *framboises* were beyond reproach. He added a little more cream.

The word ESTRAGON meant only one thing. There must be an emergency of some kind.

It couldn't be anything personal. He'd telephoned Doucette just before dinner. She'd been in the middle of her favourite serial and he'd had to do battle against background music from the television. In any case, if it was something personal surely the telephone would have sufficed.

In all his time with *Le Guide* the use of the emergency codeword had been minimal. The last occasion he could recall had been all of two years ago when Truffert from Normandy had been caught reading a copy of *L'Escargot*, *Le Guide*'s staff magazine, while reporting on a restaurant in Nice. There had been hell to pay. Anonymity was a sacred rule, never to be broken. Heads had rolled.

But then its use had been in reverse; a call to Headquarters from someone in the field. He couldn't recall a time when the word had gone out from Headquarters itself. He wondered if it was a general alarm. Perhaps all over France colleagues were waiting for their *café* as he was and wondering.

The first cup came and went. Declining a second, he rose and made his way towards the door. As he did so he caught the eye of the blonde girl. She blushed and looked down at her plate as if conscious that he'd singled her out for attention.

On his way out he passed two more tables whose occupants were having to make a fresh decision over the last course, just as he had done. They didn't look best pleased either. The maître d'hôtel probably wouldn't thank him if he paused and recommended the *framboises*—even though they were probably the best he'd ever tasted. They would need all their supplies that evening. To have one dish off was bad enough. To run out of a second would be little short of disaster.

In the foyer he looked for a public telephone booth. It wouldn't do to use the telephone in his room and risk being overheard—not until he knew what it was all about. Despite the fact that it was an automatic dial-out system, he had an old-fashioned mistrust of hotel telephones.

He emptied his change on to a shelf, fed some coins into the machine and dialled his office number. It was answered on the first ring.

'Ah, Monsieur Pamplemousse.' It was a voice he didn't recognise. Normally he didn't have much contact with the night shift. '*Monsieur le Directeur* is expecting you. *Un moment.*'

The Director was even quicker off the mark than the switchboard girl. He must have been sitting with his hand permanently on the receiver.

'Pamplemousse? Are you all right? What kept you?'

'I'm afraid the *café* was a little slow in arriving, *Monsieur.*'

'*Café!*' There was a noise like a minor explosion at the other end. 'You stopped for *café?*'

'*Oui, Monsieur le Directeur.*' Monsieur Pamplemousse decided he must proceed with care. The tone was not friendly. 'In view of the gravity of your message I felt it wise not to arouse suspicions by leaving my table with too great a haste.'

'Ah!' The response was a mixture of emotions, of incredulity and suspicion giving way, albeit with a certain amount of reluctance, to grudging respect. 'Good thinking, Pamplemousse. Good thinking.'

Monsieur Pamplemousse breathed a sigh of relief. It was often a case of thinking on one's feet with the Director. Like a boxer, you needed constantly to anticipate.

'How was your meal?' From the tone of the other's voice it was clear he regarded the answer as a foregone conclusion. Not for the first time Monsieur Pamplemousse found himself marvelling at the efficiency of *Le Guide*. He wondered how the news from Les Cinq Parfaits had got through so quickly. It was almost uncanny at times. He had a mental picture of the Operations Room; the illuminated wall-map, the large table in the centre of the room with its little flags to represent the Inspectors. The girls with their long sticks moving them around. The shaded lights. The staff talking in hushed voices as the reports came in. However, tonight was no normal night.

'It left a lot to be desired, *Monsieur*. Particularly towards the end.'

'This is a disaster, Aristide. A disaster of the first magnitude.'

'It was not good news, *Monsieur*,' Monsieur Pamplemousse replied carefully, picking his way through the minefield of the Director's mind. 'It was not good news at all. As you can imagine, I had been looking forward to it. Perhaps,' he tried to strike a cheerful note, 'perhaps it only goes to show that nothing in this world can ever be wholly perfect.' Encouraged by the silence at the other end, Monsieur Pamplemousse began to enlarge on this theme. The Director was in an overwrought state. He had probably been working too hard. He needed soothing. 'One *soufflé* doesn't make a summer, *Monsieur*. There will be others.'

There was a long pause. 'Have you been drinking, Pamplemousse?'

'Drinking, *Monsieur*? I had an apéritif before the meal—a Kir—followed by a glass or two of Sancerre with the *Omble*, then a modest Côte Rôtie, a glass of Beaumes-de-Venise with the sweet. I forewent a liqueur . . .'

'Do you know why I sent you a telex?'

'Because of the *Soufflé Surprise, Monsieur*?'

'No, Pamplemousse.' The voice at the other end reminded him suddenly of a dog barking. 'It was *not* because of the *Soufflé Surprise*.' There was another pause, a longer one this time. 'And then again, yes, you are quite right. It *was* because of the *Soufflé Surprise*.'

Monsieur Pamplemousse decided to stay silent. Clearly he had, albeit unwittingly, scored some kind of point. Bonus points in fact. Throwing caution to the wind he edged the door to the telephone booth open a little with his foot. The heat inside was adding to the confusion in his mind. The Director's voice when he spoke again was tinged with a new respect.

'Your time with the Sûreté was not wasted, Aristide.'

'*Merci, Monsieur*. I like to think not.'

'You have a knack of going straight to the heart of the problem. Clearing a pathway through the jungle. It is indeed fortunate that we chose to send you to Les Cinq Parfaits at this moment in time. Pamplemousse . . .' The Director paused and Monsieur Pamplemousse instinctively braced himself for the next words. 'Pamplemousse, if I were to ask you for your definition of the words "liquid gold", what would it be?'

Feeling himself on safe ground at long last, Monsieur Pamplemousse didn't hesitate. 'It would be a Sauternes, *Monsieur*. A Château d'Yquem. Probably the '45. I am told that the '28 and the '37, although still wonderful, are now sadly past their best. In '45 there was an early harvest . . .'

'Aristide.' There was a hint of pleading in the Director's voice, as if he was trying to convey some kind of message. 'Aristide, I have to tell you that this is a very serious matter. Think again.'

Monsieur Pamplemousse considered the matter for a moment. He wondered if the Director was trying to catch him out. Perhaps he was thinking of a German Eiswein—the capital made out of what in other circumstances, other areas, would have been a disaster; wine made from juice which had been squeezed from grapes frozen on the vine. That could be called liquid gold indeed. He racked his brains as he tried to think of famous years when it had happened.

'Am I getting warm, *Monsieur*?'

'No, Pamplemousse.' There was an audible sigh from the other end. 'You are not getting warm. You are cold. But your temperature at this moment is nothing compared to what it will be if this problem remains unsolved. Then you will be very cold indeed. We shall *all* be very cold.'

'I have heard that the owner of Château d'Yquem holds the '67 in high regard . . .'

'Pamplemousse! Will you please stop talking about wine. It has nothing to do with wine.' Monsieur Pamplemousse fell silent as the Director's voice cut across his musings. He recognised a warning note and like a professional gambler studying the tables he decided to watch play for a while so that he could get the feel of how the numbers were running before making his next move. A moment later the wisdom of his decision was confirmed. The Director was off on another tangent.

'Do you remember the winter of '47, Pamplemousse?'

'It was a very cold winter, *Monsieur*. I was only nineteen and it was my first time away from home. I was in Paris and I remember shivering in my room and wishing I was back in the Auvergne; at least they had wood to burn there. Food was scarce and there was ice on the inside of my bedroom window.'

'There may well be ice on the inside of your bed-room window again next year, Pamplemousse, if you do not act quickly. Quickly and precisely and with the utmost discretion.

'Listen to me and listen carefully. Walls have ears as you well know, and I do not wish to repeat what I have to say.

'In four days' time you will see a red carpet being laid out on the steps of Les Cinq Parfaits, a red carpet which will stretch all the way from the entrance doors to the helicopter landing-pad at the side of the building. It is a red carpet which in its time has felt the tread of a reigning monarch of Grande-Bretagne and more than one President of the French Republic. Latterly its pile has been compressed almost beyond recovery by the weight of a man of such unbelievable wealth it is impossible to describe; a *grosse légume* who by the blessing of Allah has the good fortune to be sitting on one of the richest deposits of oil in the world.

'Each year he visits Les Cinq Parfaits as a guest of France to carry out what one might call a "shopping expedition" and at the same time indulge himself on all that is best and richest and creamiest on the menu. He is particularly partial to the *Soufflé Surprise.*'

Monsieur Pamplemousse decided to take the bull by the horns.

'With respect, *Monsieur,* I understand perfectly all that you are saying. What you are saying is that this V.I.P.—this *grosse légume* as you call him—being a guest of France, a guest of some importance to our future well-being, has to be cosseted and indulged and made to feel at home while he is here. That I understand, even if I do not necessarily approve. What I do not understand is how it affects my own stay at Les Cinq Parfaits.'

'Because, Aristide, you are *not* at this moment staying at Les Cinq Parfaits. You may think you are, but you are not. To all intents and purposes you are staying at Les Quatre Parfaits. They are a Parfait short. One of the brothers—Jean-Claude—the one who is responsible for the *soufflé* in question, has vanished. Vanished without warning and without trace.'

'That is bad news, *Monsieur,* I agree . . . but surely it is a matter for the local police . . .'

'No, Pamplemousse, it is *not* a matter for the local police. The local police must be kept out of it at all costs. There are wheels, Pamplemousse, and within those wheels there are other wheels, and within those wheels there are yet more wheels. They must all be kept oiled. Without the continuing goodwill of this *grosse légume*—and I must tell you that the speed with which he has acquired his untold wealth has not so far been matched by any show of finer feelings towards his fellow man, rather the reverse—oil will be in very short supply. It may well be diverted towards colder climes than ours.'

'But surely, *Monsieur,* if this . . . this person has to go without his *Soufflé Surprise* it is not the end of the world? Surely some other member of the staff could make one? One of the other brothers? Or if not, someone could be brought in. Girardet, perhaps? He is nearby.'

'Aristide, would you have asked Titian to paint a

Monet, or Picasso a Renoir? We are dealing with the creation of a genius.'

Monsieur Pamplemousse fell silent. The Director was right, of course. They were dealing with the product of an artist at the very pinnacle of his profession. Such things were beyond duplication.

'Pamplemousse!' The Director's voice broke into his thoughts again. 'When I say it is a serious matter, I mean it is a *very* serious matter. Who knows where it will end up? Each of the brothers is a specialist in his own right. Today there is no *Soufflé Surprise*. Tomorrow it could be the *Omble*. The day after, the *Ris de veau aux salsifis*. It is a matter that is exercising the minds of certain people at the highest levels of government. In particular of a "certain person" whose name I am not at liberty to divulge for reasons of security . . .'

'A certain person,' ventured Monsieur Pamplemousse, determined not to be outdone, 'not a million miles away.'

'No, Pamplemousse.' The Director appeared to be having trouble with his breathing again. 'A "certain person" who happens to be not two feet away from me at this very moment. Furthermore, he wishes to speak to you.'

Despite himself, Monsieur Pamplemousse stiffened as a second voice came over the phone, clear and incisive; a voice he recognised. A voice which until that moment he had only heard over the radio or on television.

'*Oui, Monsieur.*' His own voice, by comparison, sounded far away.

'*Oui, Monsieur.* I understand, *Monsieur.*

'It is a very great honour, *Monsieur.*

'Without question, *Monsieur.*'

'Now do you understand the gravity of the situation, Pamplemousse?' It was the Director again, revitalised, and showing scarcely less authority than the previous speaker. Now the voice was that of a man with a mission. The voice, Monsieur Pamplemousse couldn't help but reflect, of a man who sensed the whiff of a possible decoration somewhere close at hand. An Order of Merit, perhaps, or membership of the *Légion d'Honneur*?

'From now on you will only communicate directly with this office. The telephone will be manned day and night. The codename of your mission will be "Operation *Soufflé*". I have already spoken to Monsieur Albert Parfait. He has been instructed to render every assistance. If you require anything else, name it and it shall be yours. Otherwise, I suggest we keep conversation to a minimum.'

'*Oui, Monsieur.*'

'And Aristide . . .' The Director's voice softened for a moment. 'If . . . no, not if—*when* our mission has been brought to a successful conclusion, you may order a bottle of Château d'Yquem . . . the '45. I will see matters right with Madame Grante in Accounts. Your P39s will not be delayed. *Au revoir, et bonne chance.*'

'*Au revoir, Monsieur.*'

Monsieur Pamplemousse replaced the receiver and then stood for a few seconds lost in thought. So much for a quiet week at Les Cinq Parfaits. It was a good thing Doucette hadn't come with him as had at first been suggested. She would not have been pleased.

Gathering up the rest of his change, he pushed open the door, glancing around as he did so. He felt as though he had been inside the booth for hours and yet it could only have been a matter of minutes. Inside the restaurant itself the scene was as he had left it, the soft lights, waiters gliding to and fro, a steady hum of conversation. If only they knew what currents were developing around them.

As he crossed the entrance hall the commissionaire looked at him enquiringly and then stepped to one side. The glass doors slid quietly open for him as he drew near.

Outside the air was cool. It had a crisp feel to it; a hint of autumn. Floodlights concealed in a low wall gave a translucent glow to a bed of late-flowering roses. Nearby a fountain changed from red to green. The swimming pool beyond was deserted. Of Pommes Frites there was still no sign.

He took a silent dog-whistle from an inside pocket, placed it to his lips and blew hard several times. The result was most satisfactory. From somewhere behind the hotel pandemonium broke out; a collection of barks and howls and shrieks that would have brought a smile of satisfaction to the face of any members of the local kennel club. The shrill yelps of Papillons and Pekingese mingled with Beagles and Spaniels and did battle with Pomeranians. He recognised an Airedale or two and what sounded like a Labrador, but conspicuous by its absence was the deeper, full-throated baying of a Bloodhound answering his master's call.

It proved several things at one and the same time. The whistle was working—something he had never been totally sure about ever since he'd first bought it. It also proved that, temporarily at least, Pommes Frites was not in residence. Perhaps his huff was deeper than he'd feared, or else he'd gone off for some other reason best known to himself.

Monsieur Pamplemousse gazed gloomily at the shrubbery, hoping it might suddenly part to reveal his friend and mentor, but parting came there none.

With a heavy heart and a sense of foreboding he replaced the whistle in his pocket and, Watsonless, turned to go back inside the restaurant.

# 2

## STRANGER IN THE NIGHT

LEANING HEAVILY ON A STICK, ALBERT PARFAIT rose to his feet, pushed a large, plain bottle full of colourless liquid across his desk, then hovered uneasily as he tried to regain his balance. Unlike the bottle, which was considerably wider at the bottom than it was at the top, weight distribution was not on his side and for a moment or two it looked as though he might topple over backwards into his chair again.

Monsieur Pamplemousse resisted the temptation to go to his aid. Having been born and brought up in the Auvergne, he recognised the independence of one who also came from a mountainous region.

His restraint didn't go unrewarded. At long last Monsieur Parfait relaxed and waved his stick in a triumphant gesture which managed to embrace at one and the same time his visitor, the shadowy figures beyond the darkened glass separating his office from the kitchen, and the bottle on the table in front of him.

'*Encore!*'

Monsieur Pamplemousse obeyed with alacrity. Ordinarily he was not a great lover of *eau-de-vie*. Given the choice he would have preferred an armagnac, but the opportunity to indulge himself with another *Poire William* was not one to be missed. The somewhat depressing telephone conversation with the Director had left him feeling in need of a 'pick-me-up'.

The bottle emitted a satisfactory gurgle as he topped up his glass; the whole pear within remained tantalisingly encapsulated and unreachable. From the absence of any kind of a label he guessed Les Cinq Parfaits must make it themselves. It would be the job of the youngest recruit to slip the empty bottles over the fruit as it began to form in the late spring. Later in the year, when the pear itself was fully grown, someone else would be entrusted with the task of cutting down pear and bottle and adding the brandy. Later still, others like himself would be lucky enough to enjoy the benefit of their labours. There was a logical progression about the whole operation which appealed to his mathematical side. Truly life was not without its compensations. Just when things were looking black something unexpected happened to restore the balance. He was almost beginning to look forward to whatever fate had in store for him.

Settling back in his chair, he felt the warmth of the liquid rise up from within while he waited for his companion to speak again. The flourish of Monsieur Parfait's stick conveyed a generosity of spirit which would have been hard to resist for fear of giving offence.

He glanced around the room. High up on the wall to his right there was a framed sepia photograph. It was the original of smaller, postcard-sized versions he'd seen on sale in the entrance hall, alongside pots of home-made *confiture* and signed copies of the menu; the almost obligatory current symbols of a successful restaurant.

The photograph was of a small group posing in front of a whitewashed stone building. One of the group, the only man in fact, was in a soldier's uniform and from the way the others were dressed it must have been taken during the First World War, in the days when Les Cinq Parfaits had been known simply as Mère Parfait. Above their heads the words CAFÉ RESTAURANT were just visible, whilst to the right of a smallish window, a doorway with a bead curtain was all that separated the dining-room from the outside world.

It was far removed from the present building, which over the years had been extended, added to and improved beyond all recognition. Bead curtains had been exchanged for glass doors which opened and shut automatically at the slightest movement. Pommes Frites had caused chaos on their arrival by activating the invisible rays of the operating mechanism with his tail which was wagging furiously in anticipation of the pleasures hopefully awaited by his opposite end. The smiles in Reception had become fixed rather than welcoming.

Monsieur Parfait read his thoughts. He pointed with his stick to the sepia photograph; in the centre stood an elderly woman with her arms folded. She bore a striking resemblance to him; there was the same dark, Italian-looking skin, the same nose. She was not one to stand any nonsense.

'That was *Grand-mère*. The one in uniform was my father. He was killed only two months later—I hardly knew him. That was my mother, next to him. And that'—he singled out a small figure between the two— 'that was me. There have been many changes since those days.' He gestured towards the kitchen. 'Not the least in there. In my days it was all smoke and steam, heat and shouting. Now, it is more like a hospital. Everything is stainless steel and polished tiles and air-conditioning. There is no longer any need to shout in order to make yourself heard.'

He pointed once again to the bottle on the table. 'In my day I was like that pear; able to see the world outside, but never free to escape into it. I was a prisoner of circumstances.' He spoke without any hint of rancour, and yet Monsieur Pamplemousse couldn't help but wonder if the accompanying shrug implied regret.

Again his thoughts were read. '*Comme ci, comme ça.* You win one, you lose another. Is it better? It has to be. In the old days chefs were looked down on as the lowest of the low. There were exceptions—Carême, Brillat-Savarin, Escoffier—but they were geniuses, on a par with royalty. Many of their lesser brethren deserved to be treated the way they were.

'Nowadays, chefs are like film stars. People ask for their autographs. We have to be diplomats one moment, businessmen the next. We have to know about turnover and profit margins and cash flows. Cooking is only one of the arts we have to master.

'I tell you, inside every chef these days there is an

accountant trying to get out. Our own turnover is over ten million francs a year . . . but this year I have already spent nearly a quarter of a million francs on truffles alone. Fifty thousand has gone on flowers, two hundred thousand on laundry. Think of that! If my old grandmother knew I make more profit out of selling a signed copy of the menu than I do out of selling one of Jean-Claude's *soufflés* she would turn in her grave. As for the helicopter landing-pad—she would see that as a sign of the devil.

'*Alors!* One must move with the times. When I was small I spent all my spare moments in the kitchens. I could not have wished for better training. By the time I was fourteen I had done everything. Then I was lucky enough to be apprenticed to Fernand Point at Vienne. It was he who first inspired me to aim for the heights. For him nothing less would do; nothing was so perfect that it couldn't be improved.

'I married. My wife bore me four sons and we were blissfully happy. Then one day . . . pouf! . . . We were involved in a car crash.' He reached down and tapped his leg. 'I was lucky. I suffered nothing worse than this. But my wife was killed outright. Now I had to bring up the children. I was determined they should not only be as good as me, but better. When the time came for them to go out into the world I made sure that they, too, served their apprenticeship with a master.

'We live in an age of specialisation. If I want to buy a house I go to one lawyer. If I want to make sure when I write a cook book that I am infringing no one else's copyright, I go to another. So I sent my first son, Alain, to Barrier, where he learnt humility. It is not possible to have true greatness without a touch of humility. He is now the *saucier*. Edouard went to Bocuse, who was taught as I was, at the hands of Point. Edouard became the *rôtisseur*. Gilbert was taught by Chapel to use his imagination . . . he is now the *poissonnier* . . .'

'And Jean-Claude?'

'Ah! Jean-Claude!' Monsieur Parfait raised his eyes heavenwards. 'In life there is always an exception. Jean-Claude went his own way. He is the odd one out. He inherited his grandmother's stubbornness and, like his mother, he was born with "the gift". In his own way he is a genius, although I would not dream of telling him so—it would not be good for him. His brothers are exceptionally talented, but they have got where they are by dedication and hard work. With Jean-Claude it has always been there. He is a true "one-off"—a genuine creator. Without him we would have our three stars in Michelin, our toques and our Stocks Pots . . . but *with* him . . . who knows? His strength is that when our guests are nearing the end of their meal and feel that nothing can surprise them any more, he surpasses all that has gone before.

'One day he will take over—once he has settled down; he has the necessary qualities.

'In many ways eating at a restaurant like Les Cinq Parfaits has to be like going to a concert or reading a great novel. The opening should catch your attention and make you want to carry on. The middle must give you a feeling of inner satisfaction. After that it is necessary to have an ending which not only leaves you feeling it was all worth while, but which makes you long to return.'

'Like the *Soufflé Surprise*?'

'Like the *Soufflé Surprise*. It is, to date, Jean-Claude's

greatest creation. Ask him how he does it and he will shrug his shoulders. Pursue the matter, demand to know what secret ingredient he uses, and he will most likely laugh and change the subject. He will say, "Listen, today must be Wednesday. How do I know? Because I can hear children playing in the distance. It is their half-day." It is like asking Beethoven how he composed the Ninth Symphony when all he had in front of him was a piano and a blank sheet of paper.' Albert Parfait tapped his head. 'The "secret ingredient" is all up here.'

Monsieur Pamplemousse found himself reminded of another great restaurant—Pic of Valence. For a long time he had puzzled over the special flavour of their Kir, generously dispensed from a jug. In the end it had turned out to be nothing more complicated than an added dash of Dubonnet. Perhaps Jean-Claude's "secret ingredient" was as simple. He decided to take the plunge.

'It is because of the *soufflé* that I am here. Jean-Claude's *soufflé*—or rather the lack of it—is the cause of worry in certain quarters.'

Monsieur Parfait gave him a long, hard look. 'So I am told. *They* are worried about their *soufflé*—I am worried about my son.'

Monsieur Pamplemousse returned the look in silence. Albert Parfait's manner belied his words. They were not the actions of a worried man. Since they had met, the conversation had ranged far and wide. To say that the subject of the missing Jean-Claude had been skated around was to put it mildly. It was almost as though the other had been trying not to talk about it. If it wasn't such a bizarre notion he would have suspected that for some reason or other

**29**

Monsieur Parfait had been trying to gain time. But time for what? Being *patron* of Les Cinq Parfaits must have its headaches. By his own account the climb to the top had been long and arduous; but the higher you climb the harder you fall and it was something that could happen overnight. There were precedents.

The only sign of anxiety had been in the initial handshake. It had been firm but unexpectedly moist. And the moisture had come from within rather than without. Like the rest of the building, Albert Parfait's office was kept at an ambient temperature of 20°C.

'If you will forgive my saying so, you do not seem unduly disturbed by the news of your son's disappearance.'

'Sometimes, Monsieur Pamplemousse, appearances are deceptive. Like you, I have spent a lifetime trying to perfect the art of concealing my true feelings.'

Monsieur Pamplemousse accepted the implied rebuke with equanimity. 'You know, of course, why I am here?'

Monsieur Parfait inclined his head. 'I was informed this evening. We are very fortunate. A happy chance of fate.' He relaxed a little. 'Now that we have met I recognise you, of course. I have seen your picture many times in the newspapers. I had thought you were no longer active . . .'

'I am still called on from time to time.' Monsieur Pamplemousse got the remark in quickly before the other had time to enlarge on the cause of his early retirement. It always left him feeling he'd been put at a slight disadvantage. The word 'Follies' seemed to bring out the worst in people; add to it evocative words like 'chorus' and 'girls' and there was no holding them. It was like trying to convince a collector of taxes of the need to research a handbook on refrigeration in the South of France. If he'd been caught *dans le costume d'Adam* in the Himalayas it would have been a nine-day wonder in the *Bombay Times* and then forgotten about. In the dressing-room of the Follies—never.

'We thought at first you were from one of the guides. A man eating on his own at Les Cinq Parfaits is a rare occurrence. When we see him testing a little here . . . savouring a little there . . . choosing a table where he has a good view of all that is going on around him . . . we begin to wonder. Alain thought you were from Michelin, but then we found you had Pirelli tyres on your car, so that was out. Edouard was all for Gault Millau—especially when you called for a second helping of *Omble*. It was the dog that bothered me. It didn't fit. No one from a guide, I reasoned, would bring a dog. Now I understand. He is your . . . assistant?'

Monsieur Pamplemousse nodded. 'We are rarely parted. He has been instrumental in helping me reach some of my most memorable decisions.' In culinary terms it was true; it was hard to picture being without Pommes Frites. He wondered what Albert Parfait would say if he knew their true identity. That would give him cause to perspire.

He'd had no idea he'd been the centre of so much attention. He must be more careful in future. Perhaps at the next quarterly meeting he would put forward the suggestion that all Inspectors should be accompanied by a suitable companion. There might even be a pool of 'suitable companions' for all occasions. That would bring a flush to Madame Grante's cheeks.

'If you need to bring him inside—if there are important trails to follow—please do. I rely on your discretion. It wouldn't do for the other guests to think you are a favoured customer.'

'Rest assured, Monsieur Parfait, neither Pommes Frites nor I will abuse your trust. As for trails, time alone will tell, but we will try and keep them to a minimum. I gather the local police have not yet been informed?'

'Thankfully, no. We do not want their great boots tramping all over the hotel. It would be bad for the ambience. This way is much better. With luck, no one need ever know.'

Monsieur Pamplemousse forebore to say that without a large measure of good luck everyone would know. It would be in all the *journaux*.

'When did you last see your son?'

'This morning at around eight o'clock. When I returned from the market in Thonon. He said he was planning to visit a supplier up in the mountains. There is a monastery where they make *Fruits du vieux garçon*—the fruits of the confirmed bachelor. The name always appealed to Jean-Claude.'

'He went by car? There have been no reports of an accident . . . a breakdown perhaps?'

'He would have done—it is a long journey, but his car is still in the garage. He must have changed his mind.'

'Then he can't have gone far. Unless he went somewhere by train and got delayed. Where is the nearest station?'

'Evian. I have enquired there. No one has seen him.'

'Can you think of any reason why he would disappear? Anything that would take him away from home without telling anyone?'

Again there was a slight, barely perceptible hesitation. 'What reason could there possibly be?'

He wasn't answering the question, but Monsieur Pamplemousse decided to try another tack. 'He lives on the premises?'

'All my sons do. Alain, Edouard and Gilbert are married and they live in separate houses in the grounds. Jean-Claude and I both have apartments in the main building.'

'And he had no worries?'

'None that I know of. He is not one to talk about his problems anyway. Life for him is for living. He is always bouncing back for more.'

'And it has never happened before?'

'He has his work. He is a professional. He would not wish to let others down.'

'May I see his apartment?'

'If you think it will help.'

'At this stage anything will help.'

'I will have you shown there.' Monsieur Parfait took a firm grasp of his stick and glanced at a clock on his desk. 'If you will forgive me I will leave you to your own devices. In my profession one also has to be something of an actor. There is a performance to be put on every evening, not once, but several times over. The customers will be expecting me to make my rounds.'

'I am told that later this week you have one of your more difficult audiences arriving,' said Monsieur Pamplemousse.

'Please do not remind me.' Albert Parfait made a face. 'It is not a task I relish. Already the advance guard are here. You may have seen their caravans beyond the wood. On Friday it will be the whole entourage. I cannot begin to describe the problems they bring with them. If I tell you that last year some members of the bodyguard were caught trying to roast a whole sheep in one of the chalets it will give you an inkling. Can you imagine—they stay at Les Cinq Parfaits and they want to do their own cooking!'

'It is hard to picture.' He wondered what sort of symbol they might concoct for *Le Guide*. An upside-down lamb on a spit, perhaps—with a red cross superimposed to show that it was *interdit*? Michelin would be in their element.

'Would it not be possible one year to be *complet*?'

Monsieur Parfait took an even tighter grasp of his stick and for a brief moment allowed his true feelings to surface. 'It would be perfectly possible,' he said bitterly. 'It is also very tempting. But if you were to rephrase the question—if you were to ask me "would it be wise?", then almost certainly the answer is no. There would be repercussions. *Entre nous*, it would offend too many people. People who have long memories. There are, shall we say, wheels within wheels.'

Monsieur Pamplemousse pondered the remark before answering. It was the second time that evening the point had been made.

"And they require oiling?"

'There are many things in life which are helped on their way by a little lubrication,' said Monsieur Parfait simply. 'And there are some that would grind to a halt without it. Oil has many uses. It helps make the world go round and it soothes troubled waters. Our own waters would become turbulent indeed if I chose to be difficult. Once upon a time I might have done, but now, if I am honest, I am too old to be bothered. Besides, I have the future of my sons to consider.'

He reached for a bell-push. 'Now, I must attend to work. I wish you—I wish all of us—*bonne chance*.'

Monsieur Pamplemousse drained the glass and then picked up his book and rose to join Parfait at the door. 'I will do my best. I cannot do more.'

'If you require anything—anything at all, please let me know.'

The handshake accompanying the remark was as firm as it had been earlier. It was also perfectly dry. The *moment critique*, if there'd been one, had passed.

There was a knock at the door.

'*Entrez*.' Monsieur Parfait issued his instructions briefly to one of the two coal-black Sudanese bell-boys who normally ministered to the needs of arriving guests, then relaxed his grip on Monsieur Pample-mousse's hand. '*A bientôt*.'

'*A tout à l'heure*.'

As he followed the boy down a long, deeply car-peted corridor lined on either side with bowls of freshly cut flowers and hung with discreetly inoffensive paint-ings, Monsieur Pamplemousse was conscious of a pair of eyes boring into the back of his head. Under the pretext of blowing his nose, he paused and half-turned. He was just in time to catch Albert Parfait disappearing into his office. Clearly he had other matters to attend to before he began his tour of the dining-room.

Was it his imagination or had there been some-thing furtive about the way he moved? Furtiveness, along with some other element he couldn't quite put his finger on. Alarm, perhaps? Guilt? He filed the episode away in the back of his mind for future reference.

Outside, as they made their way along a short path which led past the restaurant towards the residential area in an adjoining building, he was aware of other eyes watching his progress. He wondered which of the diners had set off the alarm. He had an uneasy feeling that someone other than the *patron* of Les Cinq Parfaits had been responsible for passing on the news that Jean-Claude had gone missing. It was almost as if Albert Parfait would rather the fact hadn't been made known. Perhaps the turbulent waters he'd spoken of earlier contained undercurrents not yet revealed; care would have to be taken if he was to avoid getting caught up in them.

The air was heavy with the fragrance of late flowers; the beds on either side of the path were immaculately cared for. He could hear the soft swish, swish of a sprinkler somewhere close at hand. There was a louder splash from the direction of the pool. Someone must have decided to have an after-dinner swim. He hoped that whoever it was hadn't eaten as well as he had. They might never surface again. Turning a corner, he found himself instinctively looking for Pommes Frites.

The bell-boy, trained to anticipate everyone's wishes before they were even voiced, pointed towards a wooded area behind the hotel. 'He may be over there, *Monsieur*. I saw him heading that way earlier this evening.'

Monsieur Pamplemousse grunted. If Pommes Frites had gone 'wooding' there was no knowing when he would be back. Woods held a fatal fascination for Pommes Frites; probably because he spent most of his off-duty hours in Montmartre, where the nearest thing to a wood was the vineyard in rue Saint Vincent.

'He is a nice dog, that one.' The bell-boy's face suddenly split open from ear to ear in a wide smile. Pommes Frites had obviously not been idle; he had acquired a new friend. Pommes Frites was good at acquiring friends in the right places. No doubt he had also made his presence known to the kitchen staff and certain of the waiters as well. The boy's next words confirmed his suspicions.

'He also has a very good appetite. *Pouf! Sapristi!*'

'He can hold his own.'

'He should take care.' The bell-boy pointed towards the woods again. 'That is where the *bicots* are living. They do not like dogs. They are *fouillemerdes*.' Clearly he considered himself a million light years removed from the occupants of a small group of caravans whose rooftops were just visible between a gap in the trees.

Monsieur Pamplemousse looked at him with interest. *Fouillemerdes* was a word he'd only ever heard used to describe people who leafed through books on the stalls along the banks of the Seine in Paris; for this reason the wares were almost always covered in plastic. As they finally stopped by a door and the boy felt for his keys, Monsieur Pamplemousse glanced uneasily towards the woods. Pommes Frites was well able to look after himself, but all the same he resolved to look for him again at the earliest opportunity.

'They come here every year?'

'Every year.' The boy turned his key in the lock. 'As soon as the holidays are over.'

'The same people?'

'They are all the same, *Monsieur*.'

'How long do they stay?'

'A few days. That is all. Long enough.'

Monsieur Pamplemousse considered the reply. He seemed to have struck a no-go area. Long enough for what? he wondered. The smile on the boy's face had disappeared and he seemed suddenly ill at ease.

Monsieur Pamplemousse decided not to press the matter further for the time being. Instead, he tried a shot in the dark. As he pushed open the door he felt inside his wallet and took out a note.

'Thank you for your trouble. I shall be grateful if you would keep an eye on Pommes Frites for me. Make sure no harm comes to him.'

He hoped he hadn't given too much. The boy had the natural dignity of the Sudanese, and he didn't wish to cause offence.

But he needn't have worried. He was rewarded by an even larger display of white teeth. '*Oui, Monsieur*. It will be a pleasure.'

As the door clicked shut, Monsieur Pamplemousse set to work, quickly and professionally. It was quite like old times. He had no idea what he was looking for. He was simply obeying an instinct, fulfilling a need for some kind of action. It had to begin somewhere and he needed to create a picture in his mind of the person he was looking for.

There were three doors, one in each wall. He tried the one on his left. It opened on to a large cupboard. Inside there hung a row of coats and jackets. He looked at the labels; they were predictably expensive—Yves St. Laurent, Pierre Cardin. The shoes laid out neatly on a rack below were equally fashionable; mostly hand-made from Lobb of London. Albert Parfait was right—chefs did indeed enjoy a new status in society. A pair of Rossignol V.A.S. racing skis stood upright in one corner; some ice-skates hung alongside them.

The bathroom was neat and orderly. A Braun Micron de Luxe electric razor was laid out ready for use beside the washbasin. An electric toothbrush, also Braun, was clipped to the dark-blue tiles above it. Everything had its home. A large inset mirrored cabinet contained a selection of sprays and lotions.

The third door opened on to a large living-room, which in turn led into a bedroom. On one side there was a long picture-window. He drew the curtains carefully and then turned on the lights. An open hatch revealed the kitchen area.

The living-room itself was simple, even austere. It was the unlived-in room of a bachelor who spent most of his time either working or out doing other things.

He wondered what Holmes would have made of it. Probably from a few hastily crushed cigarette-ends in an ashtray and signs of pacing to and fro on the carpet, he would have built up a complete picture, astounding Watson and solving the mystery at one and the same time. However, there were no ashtrays and the beige carpet looked as fresh as the day it was first laid.

He drew a blank in the kitchen. It echoed the tidiness of the bathroom. There were more gadgets, a whole battery of them, ready and waiting. Jean-Claude must be a gadget salesman's dream. A Moulinex juicer stood in pieces on the draining-board, its inside stained orange from carrot juice. He wondered whether the owner suffered from bouts of indigestion like himself, or whether he simply liked carrots. Probably the latter. The refrigerator was stocked up with bottles of Evian water. Living where he did he could hardly drink anything else.

He went back into the living-room. There was a notable absence of books apart from a row on a shelf above the desk, mostly to do with work and winter sports. The television was Sony; the video beneath it the latest Betamax. Fixed to the wall was a Bang & Olufsen Beosystem 3000; underneath that a rack of L.P.s. Somewhat to his surprise they were mostly big bands: Basie, Ellington, Buddy Rich, with a sprinkling of older groups—Lionel Hampton, Mugsie Spanier, Benny Goodman.

He found himself warming to Jean-Claude. They were on common ground at last. Perhaps one day they would be able to get together and exchange notes. Doucette didn't approve of his taste in music and complained when he had it on too loud. He envied Jean-Claude his freedom to turn up the volume when he felt like it. Big bands needed a big band sound.

There was a disc by Ben Webster and Art Tatum already on the turntable. It was one he hadn't come across before. The remote controller was on a table near the window. Unable to resist the temptation he pressed the switch. The sound of 'All the Things You Are' gave him an instant lift.

He skimmed through the bedroom, feeling under the mattress, briefly checking the cupboard drawers. There was nothing worthy of comment. It was all high-tech monastic. On a table beside the double-bed a matt-black Italian Stilnoro lamp illuminated a Nordmende clock-radio. The alarm was set for six o'clock. There was also a cordless telephone—the kind with the dialling buttons in the handset, and a small pile of magazines—mostly to do with food and drink. They looked untouched. There was also a catalogue from Sports-Schuster of Munich showing the latest in skiing equipment and clothing. Several items were marked. Jean-Claude must have been making plans for the coming winter season. He didn't look like a man with too many problems.

He returned to the living-room and switched on the quartz-halogen lamp on the desk. A larger version of the bedroom lamp, the low voltage bulb produced a brilliant white light. He picked up the blotting pad and held it under the lamp. Jean-Claude was a doodler on the phone. It was covered with black, geometrical shapes, ranging in complexity from mere squares and triangles to complex, ornate patterns—probably depending on the length of the call. Interspersed with the patterns were telephone numbers. He checked with the handset. They were mostly Jean-Claude's own number, but here and there were others. Taking out his notepad, he jotted these down for future reference.

He turned the blotting pad over. Someone—an executive working for Burns, the big American agency—had once told him that the first thing he did when he was left alone in an office belonging to anyone of importance was to look beneath the blotting pad. In a security-conscious age, when more and more code-numbers had to be committed to memory, people sought refuge by inscribing them on the back of their blotting pads. His friend had built up quite a dossier of useful numbers.

There was nothing on the back of Jean-Claude's blotting pad.

He drew a blank with the drawers on his right. The large drawer with its suspended files on the left took a little longer, but was equally unproductive.

He riffled through the books on the shelf above the desk. Nothing fell out.

Just as he was about to give up, he leant on the blotting pad, smoothing the rough paper thoughtfully with his fingers as he tried to make up his mind what to do next. It felt thicker than he would have expected. Towards the middle there were distinct ridges. He lifted the top sheet. Underneath it was a glossy black and white enprint of a blonde girl. It was the product of a fashion-conscious studio; all high-key lighting and with the softness of the subject burnt out. It made her look old beyond her years, but perhaps that was what she had wanted. She looked vaguely familiar and he wondered if he had seen her on television. The picture was unsigned; the back was stamped with the name of a studio in Geneva.

Underneath the photograph there was a thin manila envelope. It was unsealed and to his surprise, when he held it up and shook the contents on to the desk, a selection of words fluttered down. They were of differing type-sizes and faces, each separately stuck to a sheet of dark backing paper. He laid them out in no particular order. They were in English and judging by the texture of the paper had been cut from a *journal* of some kind. Strangely, at least two of the words were misspelt—unless his command of the English language, which wasn't good, was even weaker than he'd thought.

Monsieur Pamplemousse sat staring at the words for some time, shifting them around, trying to make some kind of sense. Then he stood up and tucked them back in the envelope along with the photograph. It was a task better carried out in his own room.

A few moments later he let himself out quietly through the front door. Clouds from the distant mountains had descended while he'd been at work and it was already dark. Concealed coloured lights made patches of shrubs and flowers stand out like tropical islands. The pool was deserted again. From the car-park he could hear voices and the sound of engines being revved. Doors slammed. He looked in through the dining-room windows, wondering if he should confer with Albert Parfait, but the *patron* was nowhere in sight. He decided against searching him out. It could wait for the time being.

He hesitated for a moment or two, wondering whether to take his things back to his room or look for Pommes Frites first. In view of his previous experience with the silent dog-whistle he decided not to risk using it again. All hell might break loose.

The wood behind the hotel was even darker than he'd anticipated and he began to wish he'd fetched a torch from his car. The paved path ended abruptly and gave way to gravel, then became softer still in a carpet of pine-needles. The shadows closed in almost at once, enveloping him like a shroud. Through gaps in the trees he could see occasional flashes of light from the caravans and there was a smell of something indefinably aromatic burning.

He stopped for a moment in order to get his bearings, allowing his eyes to accustom themselves to the darkness. As he did so he became aware of a movement a little way ahead and to his left; a glimpse of something white at head-height, then blackness again.

He called out, but there was no reply. Taking his belongings in his left hand, he moved forward slowly and gently with his right hand outstretched, zig-

**43**

zagging slightly as he went. He could feel his heart beating a little faster and in spite of the coolness of the night air he felt beads of sweat on his brow.

Suddenly he sensed another movement immediately in front of him and heard a stifled gasp intermingled with heavy breathing and a strange, soft, sucking sound. Easing forward he felt warmth too. The warmth of another human being, accompanied by a sweet, almost overpoweringly sickly smell.

Stretching out his hand he drew in his breath sharply as it encountered something large and round and hard. He moved it to the right and almost immediately found a second mound, similar in shape, one of a matching pair; equally hard and yet at the same time warm and soft to the touch and covered in the softest down. A mound which even as he touched it rotated as if seeking him out, rejecting and accepting at the same time. A mountain of flesh which rose and fell and became soft and moist before culminating in a peak of hardness the like of which he had never before experienced. The whole effect was so earthy, so basic, so primitively sensual, he felt rooted to the spot, unable to believe his senses.

It could only have lasted a second or two. The next moment he found himself clutching at empty air as the person he'd been touching uttered a second strangled cry, brushed past him and was gone.

Caught off-balance and still recovering from the shock of his encounter, Monsieur Pamplemousse turned and called out. But he was too late.

He started to give chase, but after only a few yards his foot met with something large and unyielding lying directly across his path. He tripped, staggered forward, and in trying to regain his balance toppled over.

As he slowly recovered his wind, Monsieur Pamplemousse opened one eye and peered at the object lying alongside him. Even in his semi-dazed state it had a familiar look about it. Opening his other eye he took a closer look. He needed no light to aid his identification. He knew at once what it was.

Stretched out on a pile of old newspapers, stiff and motionless, cold to the touch, lay the recumbent form of Pommes Frites.

# 3

## A Cause for Celebration

For a moment or two there was silence as Monsieur Pamplemousse remained where he'd fallen, trying to get his breath back, while at the same time weighing up the pros and cons of applying the kiss of life to Pommes Frites. Finally, having decided to take the plunge, he leaned forward. Desperate situations demanded desperate measures.

Monsieur Pamplemousse yielded to no one in his love for Pommes Frites. Deep down he knew that had the situation been reversed there would have been no hesitation about coming to his aid. Nevertheless, the prospect of mouth-to-mouth resuscitation was not one he relished. Pommes Frites had a generous nature and in return nature had endowed him with lips to match. Even the famous Westmores of Hollywood might have admitted to having met their match had they been called upon to make him up for the part of a canine Scrooge; Max Factor would have had to work overtime.

All that aside, when he finally screwed up his courage and lifted one of Pommes Frites' lips in order to begin work, Monsieur Pamplemousse discovered that it was not only very large and wet, it also had a most peculiar taste: an amalgam of flavours, some relatively fresh, others obviously deeply ingrained. The overall effect was, to say the least, uninviting, and with a view to tempering necessity with expediency, coupled with a desire to get the whole thing over as quickly as possible, he blew rather harder than he'd intended.

The result was electrifying. Pommes Frites leapt to his feet and gave vent to a long-drawn-out shuddering howl. At least, to be pedantic and strictly for the record, he opened his mouth and emitted a noise which another member of the family *canidae* would have recognised at once for what it was: not so much a howl as a cry of surprise, pain and indignation all rolled into one. It embodied such intensity of feeling that had they been situated higher up the mountains, in the vicinity of Mont Blanc, for example, or Chamonix, it would have caused any St. Bernard who happened to be on night-duty to drop everything and come running with a keg of brandy round its neck at the ready.

Fortunately, only Monsieur Pamplemousse himself was there to hear it, and for a moment he was convinced that he had been a party to, perhaps even the cause of, the early demise of his closest and dearest friend. It was not a happy thought.

For a split second dog and master stared at one

another, each busy with his own thoughts. Then Pommes Frites relaxed. To say that he wagged his tail would have been to overstate the case. He made a desultory attempt at wagging. His brain sent a half-hearted message in that direction, but it never reached its destination. Other factors intervened en route; 'road-up' signs proliferated, diversions abounded. Not to put too fine a point on it, Pommes Frites was feeling distinctly under the weather.

It was a simple case of cause and effect. The cause wouldn't have needed a Sherlock Holmes to trace, and the effect was there for all to see—or it would have been had low clouds not been obscuring the moon.

Basically it had to do with the nature of Les Cinq Parfaits. Les Cinq Parfaits was many things to many people; the one claim it could not make was that of being the kind of restaurant where the clients made a habit of wiping their plates clean at the end of each course with large hunks of *baguette*. Bread, home-made, freshly baked, and of unimpeachable quality, was dispensed freely at the start of each meal, but sad to relate most of it remained uneaten.

Sauces, on the whole, were not mopped up. They were either consumed with the aid of the appropriate implement or they were left on the plate, along with much of the food they had been intended to comple-ment. The reason was not because the clientèle were any more polite or well-mannered than in lesser estab-lishments; it was simply that a great many of them were past their best as trenchermen. Age had taken its toll, digestive systems ruined by overwork ren-dered them incapable of taking full advantage of the pleasures they were now well able to afford, whilst in the case of the wives, sweethearts or mistresses accompanying them, they were swayed by vanity and the need to keep a watchful eye on waistlines.

The net result was that each day large quantities of rich food which had taken a great deal of time and energy and manpower to grow and to harvest, to transport and then to prepare for the table, found their way back to the kitchens untouched by knife and fork. Once there, such were the standards set by Monsieur Albert Parfait, it was immediately and unceremoniously consigned to a row of waiting swill-bins for onward delivery next day to a local pig farm whose residents had no such problems.

It was one such bin, overflowing with riches, that Pommes Frites, taste-buds inflamed through watching his master's antics on the other side of the dining-room window, his pride seriously injured, his stomach echoing like a drum, stumbled across in his wanderings earlier that evening. It had proved to be a veritable cornucopia of a swill-bin.

Pommes Frites had lost no time in getting down to serious work. The niceties of menu-planning went by the board, the ambience of his surroundings passed unnoticed. Rules for following fish by meat rather than vice versa were disregarded. There was no dilly-dallying between courses. International preferences concerning the priority of cheese over sweet were solved by the simple expedient of eating both together. Coffee was taken ad hoc.

Alphabetically, but otherwise in no particular order, he consumed in a remarkably short space of time: *Andouillette; Boeuf* prepared in a variety of ways; *Boudins*, black and white; *Caviar* (white, from the roe of the albino sturgeon); *Coq au Vin* and

*Coquilles St. Jacques* followed by *Crêpes Suzettes*. *D'Agneau sur le grill* rapidly became *d'Agneau dans le Pommes Frites*, along with *Ecrevisse; Estouffade* (cooked in the local manner with red wine, bacon and mushrooms); *Foie gras; Frâises; Fromages* too numerous to list; *Glaces* in profusion; *Gratinées; Homard*—both lukewarm and cold; *Ile flottante; Jambon; Journaux; Knackwurst* (ordered in advance by a guest from Alsace who was celebrating his birthday not wisely but too well); *Lapereau; Loup en croûte; Mousse au chocolat; Noisette de Chevreuil* served with *morilles; Oeufs* from many different sources; *Omble; Pâté; Pâtisseries;* pieces of plastic; *Pigeonneau; Pommes; Poulet; Quenelles Nantua; Queues d'écrevisses; Ris de veau; Rouget; Salade* which had once been green but was now a greyish brown; *Sorbets* in a *panaché* to end all *panachés; Truffes; Truite; Ursuline; Vacherin; Veau Waffelpasteta* (another indulgence of the guest from Alsace, most of which he'd left for fear of not living to celebrate another birthday); *Xavier* soup; *Yaourt* and *Zébrine*.

He was now suffering the after-effects of this gargantuan meal; a meal which would have caused even the great Escoffier, accustomed as he must have been to preparing vast banquets for Kings and Queens and Princes the world over, to turn in his grave and reach for the indigestion tablets.

Presented with a break-down of the contents of Pommes Frites' stomach, no self-respecting vet would have given overmuch for his chances of surviving the night, let alone of making an early recovery; a medical opinion with which the patient would have wholeheartedly concurred.

Pommes Frites couldn't remember ever having felt

quite so full before, or so under par. And it was at that moment in time that Monsieur Pamplemousse, concerned by the expression of unrelieved woe on his friend's face, unwittingly administered the unkindest cut of all. Feeling inside his jacket pocket, he produced what in normal circumstances would have been the panacea for all ills, and held the object to Pommes Frites' nose.

The effect was as devastating and immediate as had been his attempt a few moments earlier to administer the kiss of life.

Pommes Frites stared at the bone-shaped biscuit as if he could hardly believe his eyes and then, having lifted up his head and given voice to a howl which was, if possible, even more desolate than the first, tottered round in a barely completed half-circle, gazed up at his master with a look of mute despair, and then collapsed in an untidy heap on the *journal* at his feet.

Unaware of the cause of this strange behaviour, Monsieur Pamplemousse sprang into action. Clearly he couldn't leave Pommes Frites where he was. Equally clearly, Pommes Frites was in no condition to do anything about the matter himself, even if he'd wanted to.

He looked round desperately but unavailingly for help. Room service at Les Cinq Parfaits was impeccable. Pool service could not be faulted. Call for a Kir Royale and it was on the table by your side, ice-cold and with an assortment of nuts and other goodies, before you had time to call for the sunshade to be adjusted. He had a feeling though that wood service, in particular the discreet removal of a large Bloodhound to a place of comfort, might be stretching things a little too far. Bell-pushes for summoning aid were conspicuous by their absence from nearby trees.

It was then that he remembered the wheelbarrow. He'd seen it soon after his visit to Jean-Claude's room. Large, pneumatically tyred, propped against a wall alongside a bale of hay; it would be ideal.

Fetching it took only a minute or two; getting Pommes Frites inside a great deal longer. Pommes Frites was not in one of his most co-operative moods. In fact, quite the reverse. A disinterested spectator, one with no particular axe to grind, could have been forgiven had he or she jumped to the conclusion that Pommes Frites was positively against the whole operation. Not that he showed any active sign of resistance. It was simply that he did nothing to help. Even the vast amount he had eaten that evening didn't account for the fact that he suddenly felt twice his usual fifty kilograms. Limbs which normally propelled him with ease about his daily rounds became weak and useless, unable to support his weight. His head, normally erect and with a certain nobility about it, lolled from side to side, eyes rolling in their sockets, tongue hanging loose, as if he was suffering from some dreadful and incurable mental affliction.

Three times Monsieur Pamplemousse nearly succeeded in his task, and three times when he tried to turn the barrow upright Pommes Frites rolled out the other side, landing heavily on the ground with his paws in the air.

Fourth time lucky, conscious that sartorially speaking he was far from looking his best, Monsieur Pamplemousse set off at long last on the journey back to his room. As he turned a corner leading to the final stretch he heard voices and paused. Doubling back on himself he tried another route which took him past the dining-room again. Adopting a shambling, crab-like movement so that he could keep his back towards the windows, he swallowed his pride and touched the brim of his hat in a suitable servile acknowledgement of the interest his activities were arousing on the other side of the glass before hurrying past as fast as his load would permit.

Reaching the door to his room he uncovered yet another deficiency of Les Cinq Parfaits. In *Le Guide*, alongside an impressive list of symbols showing the various facilities which ranged from pool-side telephones to coin-operated vibro-mattresses (on request), was one which denoted easy access for those who had the misfortune to be confined to a wheelchair. After struggling for several minutes to enter his room, Monsieur Pamplemousse came to the conclusion that any further projects designed to attract canine customers who wished to arrive in a wheelbarrow would have to remain in the pending tray for a while. Structural alterations of a major kind would be needed; doorways would have to be widened, L-shaped corridors straightened out.

His mission completed, Pommes Frites finally and safely parked in the middle of the room, Monsieur Pamplemousse collapsed on to his bed and lay where he'd fallen for some minutes while he contemplated the air-conditioning inlet above his head. At length, duty calling, he reached for the local telephone directory.

There were three *vétérinaires* listed. The first failed to answer. The second announced by means of a recorded message that he was on holiday. The third call produced in the fullness of time the sleepy voice of someone who didn't sound best pleased at being woken.

Monsieur Pamplemousse looked at his watch. He had totally lost all track of time. The hands showed a little after eleven o'clock.

He listened as patiently as possible while he was given a run-down of the other's problems, followed by a list of priorities in which attending to ailing and unregistered dogs after six o'clock in the evening appeared to enjoy low priority against ministering to any local cows who happened to have acquired inflammation of the udders.

'*Monsieur*,' he said at last. 'I do know about the *vaches d'abondance*. I realise their importance to the local economy. I know that they are gentle, brown and white creatures who enrich our lives immeasurably. I have heard the sound of the bells they wear around their necks. They have often kept me awake at night when I have been staying in the mountains. I know that without them France, indeed the whole world, would be deprived of some of its finest cheeses; the *Gruyères* of *Comté* and *Beaufort, Emmental,* the *Tommes de Savoie, Reblochon* . . .

'No, *Monsieur*, it will not be possible to bring him in tomorrow morning.' He glanced across the room at Pommes Frites. He hadn't moved. 'From the look of him he will not be going anywhere for some time to come. He has the appearance of one who has eaten a large quantity of plaster of Paris. Plaster of Paris which has now set hard . . .

'He is in a wheelbarrow, here in my room at Les Cinq Parfaits . . .

'I realise you have had a busy day, *Monsieur*. I, too, have had a busy day. I rose at six o'clock this morning. I have driven all the way from Paris and I, too, am very tired. But this is a matter of great importance and the utmost urgency . . .'

Monsieur Pamplemousse broke off in mid-sentence. He stared disbelievingly at the receiver. It was almost beyond belief but the person at the other end had actually hung up on him.

He hesitated for a moment or two, wondering whether to try again and offer a piece of his mind, or to telephone Durelle in Paris. Durelle would be more sympathetic. He also knew about Bloodhounds in general and Pommes Frites in particular. As one-time adviser to the Sûreté (*Division Chiens*) he had known Pommes Frites during his early days with the force and was well used to his ways.

In the end Monsieur Pamplemousse decided against both courses of action. It was late and Pommes Frites' breathing had become more regular. Regular and noisy. If he carried on at the present rate Les Cinq Parfaits would be liable to lose their red rocking-chair in the Michelin guide. He knew the signs. Soon the heavy breathing would turn into snores. Sleep for Monsieur Pamplemousse would become difficult, if not impossible. The way things were going he might be better off finding alternative accommodation for the night.

Several times Pommes Frites opened his mouth and licked his lips as if reliving in his dreams some recent experience of a gastronomic nature. Monsieur Pamplemousse lifted up one of his eyelids and immediately wished he hadn't. The orb which met his gaze was bloodshot rather than hazel and totally devoid of expression. A strong smell of hay had begun to fill the room; hay and damp newsprint. It was not a pleasant combination.

Dropping Pommes Frites' eyelid back into place, he essayed a few desultory tugs at the bedding and then gave it up as a bad job, resolving to leave matters in abeyance until the morning. At least Pommes Frites wasn't getting worse and there was work to be done.

Heaving a deep sigh he crossed to a desk in the corner of the room and drew up a chair. Upending the envelope he had taken from Jean-Claude's room revealed something which had escaped his notice the first time: a small cutting showing a group of skiers posing against a snow-covered mountainside. It must have been the other way up before—on the back he recognised part of a picture showing a stretch of water; it might have been anywhere. He turned the cutting over again. There were five people in the group—all male—two kneeling and three standing behind, arms akimbo. Although as a group they looked blissfully happy, he was left with a strange and irrational feeling of unease. Against the man in the middle of the back row someone had inked in a black cross and a question-mark. He held the cutting up to the light to examine it more closely. Presumably it had either been cut from a glossy magazine, or from some kind of brochure.

Putting it to one side for future reference, he turned his attention to the remaining cuttings. Something about the type-face rang a bell. In fact, he'd seen it quite recently. A loud snore from behind reminded him; a moment's comparison confirmed his suspicions. Bits of identical newsprint were sticking to Pommes Frites. They must have come from the *journal* he'd been lying on in the wood.

The odd thing was that although they looked genuine enough on the surface, many of them didn't make sense. As with the cuttings, words were misspelt, letters transposed. The whole thing was clearly a fake; it couldn't possibly ever have been a part of something seriously offered for sale to the general public. But why? For what purpose? Who would go to all the trouble of printing a mock-up of a *journal* simply to cut out particular words? Presumably they were meant to be put together at some stage to form a message, but why print the words separately to start with—why not print the entire message? And if they *had* gone to all that trouble, why not get it right? It was all so amateurish.

His senses quickened as he felt under Pommes Frites and came across another piece of newsprint from which a single word had been cut out, part of a headline which read RUSSIAN SUBMARINE . . .

A quick search through the pile of cuttings on his desk revealed the missing word: DANGRE. It was neatly pasted on to a sheet of plain paper, but when he held it underneath the gap in the original it fitted exactly.

He sat down again and counted the words. There were seventeen—none were duplicated. Gazing at them he found himself reminded of the time he'd spent in England shortly after the war. In an effort to improve his English he'd become a crossword addict, revelling in the cryptic clues and the anagrams. The present problem was like an anagram, only using words instead of letters.

He set them out in no particular order, just as he had been in the habit of doing with the crossword: OF, ONE, HURRY, MESSEGE, YOUR, DANGRE, MY, NEXT, PO-LICE, LOVED, IS, NOT, AWAAIT, DO, IN-FORM, LIFE, IN.

Mathematically the number of possible combinations was beyond his ability to calculate. At least with a crossword one could eliminate certain letters by solving other clues, either across or down. He felt a bit like the proverbial monkey sitting at a typewriter trying to prove the theory that if it kept on typing at random for long enough it would eventually come up with the complete works of Shakespeare. That kind of time, however, was not at his disposal; according to the Director he only had until Friday at the latest.

Bringing logic to bear on the problem, he tried another approach—pairing certain words with each other in the hope of reducing the number of variations: IN-FORM with POLICE, LIFE with DANGRE, LOVED with ONE, NEXT with MESSEGE.

He added AWAAIT to NEXT MESSEGE, YOUR to LOVED and ONE.

Suddenly things began to slip into place. He had a complete sentence: AWAAIT NEXT MESSEGE OF YOUR LOVED ONE.

Returning to the first two pairings, he added MY, IS and IN, and it became IN-FORM POLICE MY LIFE IS IN DANGRE, leaving him with HURRY, DO and NOT.

Laying the words out carefully in a long line Monsieur Pamplemousse reread the complete message: IN-FORM POLICE MY LIFE IS IN DANGRE. DO NOT HURRY. AWAAIT NEXT MESSEGE OF YOUR LOVED ONE.

A sense of elation came over him. He felt a sudden need to communicate his success. What was it the Director had said? My office telephone will be manned day and night. Perhaps even now he was sitting at his desk, drumming.

Reaching for the handset, Monsieur Pamplemousse pressed the appropriate button for an outside line and was halfway through dialling when he hesitated. What had he achieved? He'd pieced together a presumably as yet unsent message, albeit in double-quick time, but it hadn't got him any further. Repeated over the telephone it would sound like a non-event. It would trigger off a set of questions to which he had, as yet, no answers. Far better to sleep on the matter and allow his subconscious to do some of the work. Monsieur Pamplemousse was a great believer in the subconscious.

It had, in fact, already been at work. Even while he'd been dialling the Office number it had sent out a message reminding him of something else the Director had said; a promise made, and one which he fully intended taking advantage of. The promise of a bottle of the d'Yquem '45 when his mission had reached a satisfactory conclusion.

Deep down, Monsieur Pamplemousse was only too well aware that he had only really begun to scratch the surface of his problem, but scratches could widen into cuts, cuts into fissures, fissures into crevasses. There was no question of failure. Failure was not a word in his vocabulary; consequently it never entered his mind.

The evening had not been entirely without success. He now had things to work on. It was a cause for celebration. As a *digestif* and an aid to peaceful sleep while his subconscious got to work, he could think of nothing better than a glass or two of Sauternes.

He reached for the telephone again and pressed the button marked 'Room Service'. It was more than likely that Les Cinq Parfaits, for all the riches which graced the pages of its wine-list, riches which reached back to long before he was born, would be unable to meet his request. It was asking a lot, but it was worth a try.

'*Monsieur* is fortunate. We have only three bottles left. When they are gone we shall be reduced to the '62s.'

'Bring me two,' said Monsieur Pamplemousse in a sudden mood of recklessness. He would have one to be going on with and keep one for later, depending on the final outcome. It would help make up for a spoilt holiday and the absence of the *Soufflé Surprise* he'd been so looking forward to.

If the man was surprised there was no sign of it in his voice. It might have been the kind of order he received every night of his life. If there was any emotion at all it was one of respect; respect mingled with the faintest hint of regret.

'Perhaps,' said Monsieur Pamplemousse, 'you would care to share a glass with me as a nightcap—a little *boisson prise avant de se coucher*?'

'It would be an honour, *Monsieur*.' He knew from the tone of the man's voice that he had made a friend for life. Wine was a great leveller; a breaker-down of barriers.

The discreet knock on the door came sooner than expected. An assistant *sommelier*, still wearing his green baize apron, his badge of office—the silver *tastevin*—round his neck, entered the room pushing a trolley on which reposed two ice-buckets and two glasses. There was also a plate of wafer-thin biscuits. A palate cleanser.

Having circumnavigated Pommes Frites with scarcely more than a passing glance, he withdrew a bottle from one of the ice-buckets, holding it up with care for Monsieur Pamplemousse's inspection.

Monsieur Pamplemousse assumed a suitably reverent expression, and then watched with approval while the *sommelier* went to work. From the painstaking way in which he removed the lead foil in one piece, pressing it out flat with obvious pleasure, he guessed the man must come from his own area. Only someone from the Auvergne would go to so much trouble over something which to most people would be relatively unimportant. It was strange how different areas produced people who gravitated towards certain jobs. Half the restaurants in Paris were owned or staffed by Auvergnese. If it was a Frenchman behind the wheel of a taxi, rather than an Asian, the chances were he would be from Savoie. He resolved that when the wine was finished he would replace the foil and add the bottle to his collection, a reminder of his time at Les Cinq Parfaits. Something else for Doucette to dust, as she would no doubt tell him.

Cork withdrawn, passed below the nose in an automatic gesture, the *sommelier* ran some pieces of ice round the inside of the glasses, then dried them and began to pour. Against the white of the cloth the wine was amber-gold, tinged with yellow at the rim. It augured well. There was no sign of maderisation.

'*Monsieur*.' The *sommelier* handed him one of the glasses. Taking it by the base, Monsieur Pamplemousse held it up to the light, then down against the cloth, regarding it for a while, tilting it through forty-five degrees so that he could watch the 'legs' form on the inside. Satisfied at long last, he held the glass to his nose and savoured the rich, unmistakable, honeyed smell, powerful and concentrated.

The sweetness hit the tip of his tongue first. The flavour lingered long after the first mouthful, producing an aftertaste full of finesse and breeding.

'It is how gold should taste.'

'It will improve, *Monsieur*. A *soupçon* more of coldness.'

'I have only tasted it once before and that was in company. Never have I had a whole bottle to myself, let alone two. It is too good to drink alone.'

They stood in silence for a while, then the *sommelier* put down his empty glass with a sigh of regret.

'It is too good, *Monsieur*, for many people to drink at all. Unfortunately, in my profession one comes to realise that the best wine does not always go to those who appreciate it most.'

Pausing by the door, the man looked him straight in the eye. 'Thank you again, *Monsieur*, and ... *bonne chance*.'

Monsieur Pamplemousse pondered the remark over a biscuit. Perhaps he was being over-sensitive, but in the circumstances and considering what time it was, *bonne nuit* might have been more appropriate.

Pouring himself another glass of wine, he made his way into the bathroom. There was nothing more conducive to thought than a lingering hot bath and the notion of one enhanced by a bottle of Château d'Yquem was positively sybaritic.

But the bath produced little or no result other than an uneasy feeling that his presence at the hotel was a matter of some comment; that others knew far more than he did. Well, it wouldn't be the first time. Most of his life he'd had to battle against such things. He would get there in the end.

As he lay luxuriating in the foam from a sachet of liquid bath oil, he turned over in his mind all that had happened that evening. Memories of his strange encounter in the wood came flooding back and multiplied, aided and abetted by the warm water, Badedas and Sauternes. He began to feel strangely disturbed. Perhaps a cold shower would have done him far more good.

The towels were of the finest cotton, satisfyingly large and absorbent; there was a voluminous dressing-gown monogrammed with the hotel's initials to match.

Topping up his glass for the final time, Monsieur Pamplemousse placed the empty bottle on top of the refrigerator, consigned its companion to the compartment on the inside of the door, adjusted the temperature so that it wouldn't become over-chilled, and retired at long last to his bed. With the alarm set for eight o'clock, he fluffed up the pillows and picked up his book. Opening it at the point where he'd left off in the restaurant, he returned to *The Hound of the Baskervilles*. But reading it did not come easily. He found himself going over the same paragraph again and again; Holmes was explaining to Watson a theory he had formed about some knotty problem.

Monsieur Pamplemousse found himself wondering sleepily what the famous detective would have made of his present situation, especially the encounter in the wood. Encounters of an amorous nature didn't figure largely in Holmes' adventures. He would have taken a coldly analytical approach to the whole thing, listing all the possibilities, trying them out on the Doctor for effect.

He glanced down. His own Watson was still fast asleep, twitching every so often in his dreams. He would get no help there for the time being.

Twisting open his Cross pen, he picked up a pad of paper and began to write. For some while he wrote and scratched out and amended and cut and edited and then rewrote again, filling page after page. Not until he was completely satisfied did he lay down his pen and even then he tore up the used sheets and transferred the distillation of his findings to a fresh page before reading it out loud.

'What we are looking for,' he intoned to his captive audience of one, 'and there cannot be many in this world who fit the description, is an illiterate English female compositor, who stands about 168 centimetres tall, and is possessed of a *balcon* of such largeness and generosity, of such roundness and hardness, that it almost defies belief.'

Ignoring the snore which came from the direction of the wheelbarrow, Monsieur Pamplemousse tore the sheet off the pad and placed it carefully beneath the glass on the bedside table. Well pleased with the result of his evening's work, he turned out the light and closed his eyes.

One thing was for certain: given the opportunity, he would be able to identify them again anywhere, anytime, anyplace. They were indelibly and disturbingly etched on his memory.

He had another flash of inspiration before sleep finally overtook him. He remembered where he'd seen the subject of the photograph before. It was the girl who had been sitting all alone in the restaurant that evening.

# 4

## TAKING THE WATERS

'I AM LOOKING, *MONSIEUR*, FOR A WOMAN WITH exceptionally large *doudounes*. Large, firm and of coconut-like hardness. A woman who is not averse to exposing them to the world . . .'

'Aren't we all, Pamplemousse, aren't we all.' The Director sounded tired, as though he had been up all night. 'May I remind you that you are in the Haute-Savoie, not St. Tropez.'

Monsieur Pamplemousse decided to ignore the interruption. 'They belong,' he continued, 'to someone who works, or has worked, in the printing trade. Possibly someone who has a grudge. I am told there is a great deal of redundancy in the industry. Competition from the Orient is severe.'

'Pamplemousse!' The Director's voice cut in again. 'Why is it that whenever you are on a case there is always a woman involved? Sooner or later sex rears its ugly head. Usually it is sooner rather than later.'

'*Cherchez la femme, Monsieur*. It is my experience in life that there is always a woman involved. Man has a great and undying and unquenchable need for woman. It has been so ever since the Garden of Eden. You could say, *Monsieur*, that were I to find this woman I would be well on the way to solving the problem.'

From the silence at the other end he felt that he had scored a point, and from the length of that silence it was not just an outer or a magpie, but a bullseye; a direct hit.

'No, Pamplemousse, *I* would not say that. You are saying it. The choice of words is yours.' There was a note of acerbity in the voice, and yet Monsieur Pamplemousse felt there were also overtones of respect; respect and some other quality he couldn't quite define. A whisker of apprehension perhaps?

'May I ask you something, Aristide?' The Director was clearly about to change his tune.

'*Oui, Monsieur*.'

'It is only a small thing, of little importance I'm sure. But it kept me awake last night wondering.'

'Please ask anything you wish, *Monsieur*.'

'Why were you pushing Pommes Frites about the gardens of Les Cinq Parfaits in a wheelbarrow last night? Has he suffered some kind of injury?'

'Shall we say, *Monsieur*, that he is indisposed.'

'Nothing serious, I trust?'

Monsieur Pamplemousse glanced towards the subject of their conversation. It was hard to say. Pommes Frites hadn't visibly moved from where he'd been deposited some ten or eleven hours previously. Nev-

ertheless there was some improvement; he appeared
to be regarding the outside world through at least one
half-open, if decidedly lack-lustre eye which could
only be interpreted as a step in the right direction.
His jowls gave an occasional twitch.

'It is difficult to form an opinion, *Monsieur*.'

'You must seek medical advice.'

'I am about to phone his *vétérinaire* in Paris. It
may take time.'

'Time is not on our side, Pamplemousse.' The Director sounded agitated again. 'A "certain person"
has been on to me already this morning demanding
news of progress. I can hardly repeat what you have
just told me. I understand the workings of your mind,
Aristide. I respect them. I know that threads have to
be picked up and examined and pondered on before
you weave them together into some sort of pattern,
however bizarre and convoluted. I know that ordinarily this takes time, but I hesitate to pass on the news
that the boilers and generators of France depend for
their life's blood on a pair of *doudounes*, however
large and desirable they may be.'

'*Oui, Monsieur*.'

'Were they . . .' The voice hesitated. 'Were they
very exceptional, Aristide? Clearly, they made a deep
impression on you.'

'*Formidable, Monsieur. Extraordinaire*. I will describe the situation and the events leading up to it
more fully when I make my report.'

'Good. I shall look forward to that moment. We will
go through it over a bottle of champagne. Some of
your favourite Gosset.' The Director sounded in a
better mood. 'Now, I will leave you to your telephoning. Command the *vétérinaire* to fly down to Geneva

if necessary. We will arrange for a car to meet him. Tell him it is a matter of supreme national importance. Oil is a valuable commodity. I need hardly stress the fact that other powers are interested. Powers, Aristide, whose climate is such that their needs during the winter months are even greater than our own. Pommes Frites must be restored to the peak of condition as quickly as possible. I have a high regard for his abilities and they must not be impaired.'

Monsieur Pamplemousse murmured his goodbyes and then with a sigh replaced the receiver. He bent down to pat the wheelbarrow's occupant on the stomach. Almost immediately there was a distant rumble; a warning of worse things to come.

Monsieur Pamplemousse hastily drew the curtains and flung open a window. At least one of Pommes Frites' abilities remained unimpaired; in fact, enhanced was more the word. If he stayed where he was storm-cones would need to be hoisted over the barrow; the air-conditioning would be tested to its limits.

He stood for a moment breathing in the fresh autumn air. The distant sound of a ship's siren announced the presence of a paddle-steamer making its morning round of the lake. Waiters in jeans and sweatshirts were busy on the nearby terrace, laying the tables for lunch—holding wineglasses above a jug of steaming water before giving them a final polish. Laughing and joking amongst themselves, they looked very different to the slightly aloof figures who had attended him the night before. One of them was busy raking a patch of earth where a mark had been left by the wheelbarrow. He waved as he caught sight of Monsieur Pamplemousse.

Monsieur Pamplemousse returned the wave automatically, his mind suddenly on other things. How, for example, had the Director got to hear about the episode with the wheelbarrow quite so speedily? Someone must have been very quick off the mark in complaining. Someone high up in government, perhaps? Either that, or there was some other source of communication. Whichever it was, it left him feeling irritated.

He turned away from the window and contemplated Pommes Frites for a moment. It was not an inspiring sight. Had they been with him at that moment the powers that be in Paris would have had their confidence in the future well-being of France severely shaken.

Monsieur Pamplemousse reached for the telephone and his notebook. There were times when he felt as if he spent half his life on the phone. It was one of the penalties of working in the field. This morning was no exception. He still had all the numbers he'd found on Jean-Claude's pad to go through. In the old days, back at the Sûreté, it would have been delegated to a subordinate.

His friend Durelle, the *vétérinaire,* greeted his request with a certain amount of derision.

'Drop everything? Do you realise, in my waiting-room this morning I have seven dogs, three cats, a parrot, a tortoise, and an old woman with a budgerigar. The budgerigar is eleven years old and will live for another five or six years at least. The old woman merely needs someone to talk to other than a creature who can only say *Bonjour, Bonne nuit* and *Ooh, la, la!* She comes here every week.'

'It is a matter of national importance.'

'Are you pulling my leg?'

He didn't blame Durelle for asking. Over the years they had played a series of long-running practical jokes on each other. Childish pranks which had seemed enormous fun at the time, but which didn't always stand retelling. Like puns, they were things of the moment. There was the time when, having heard that Durelle had ordered a new suit, he had persuaded the tailor to parcel up an old sack which he'd found lying in a street, one used to divert the flow of water in one of the gutters of Montmartre until it became too old even for that. It had stunk to high heaven. Durelle had passed no comment at the time, but he'd got his own back by giving it to him as a present the following Christmas. It had gone to and fro for several years until Doucette had put her foot down.

'No, I am perfectly serious. You can check with the office. I am staying at Les Cinq Parfaits, by Lac Léman . . .'

'Lucky devil! I wish I could join you. We could do a spot of fishing together.'

'The grass is always greener on the other side of the fence,' said Monsieur Pamplemousse, slightly aggrieved. 'The way things are going I shan't have much time for fishing.'

'Has he been overeating again? I seem to remember it happening once before. That time when you were both in Normandy. Apples stuffed with quail and baked in pastry, was it not? Afterwards Pommes Frites was given the cream bowl to lick and suffered accordingly. It took him several days to recover.'

'*Chiens* are *interdits* in the dining-room at Les Cinq Parfaits,' said Monsieur Pamplemousse defensively. 'Besides, he appears to have lost his appetite completely. He turned up his nose at a biscuit I offered him, one of his favourites which I keep for special occasions. It is always a bad sign.'

'Has he been taking the local water?'

'We are staying near Evian.'

'Ah, then we must look elsewhere. Are his eyes at all bloodshot?'

'Pommes Frites' eyes are often bloodshot,' said Monsieur Pamplemousse reprovingly. 'He is, after all, a Bloodhound.'

'Yes, of course.' Durelle sounded distracted. In the background there was the noise of a dog barking. 'And his nose? Is it dry?'

'It is hard to say. It has recently been greased. I gave it a liberal coating of Vaseline before we left Paris. Enough to last the holiday.'

'Temperature?'

'Again, it is hard to say. He felt very cold to the touch last night, but he'd been lying out in a wood . . .'

'*Un moment*.' There was a pause followed by a heavy clunk as the receiver at the other end was laid down. There were now several dogs barking. It sounded like a fight. He heard a muttered oath, then a door slammed. When Durelle picked up the phone again he was breathing heavily and his words were interspersed with loud sucking noises as though he had been wounded.

'It is a bad morning. I'm truly sorry I cannot be with you.' The remark was made with feeling. 'I assume you have contacted a local vet?'

'They are not enthusiastic,' said Monsieur Pamplemousse. 'Besides, I need someone I can trust.'

'In that case I can only suggest you send me a specimen of his water for analysis.'

'Pommes Frites' water?' Monsieur Pamplemousse repeated the words dubiously.

'A few millilitres will be sufficient. If you put it on the afternoon train I will get my secretary to arrange for its collection at the Gare du Lyon. You shall have my full report first thing tomorrow morning. We will take it from there. In the meantime, if there is any change for the worse do not hesitate to ring me. I will come at once if necessary.'

Monsieur Pamplemousse replaced the receiver and eyed Pommes Frites gloomily. He foresaw difficulties. It was one thing taking a horse to the water; it was another matter entirely getting it to drink. The converse problems in Pommes Frites' case were all too obvious. Although on the surface Pommes Frites' plumbing arrangements left a lot to be desired—so much so that a passing stranger encountering him for the first time on the slopes of Montmartre might well have been forgiven had he classed them somewhere betwen 'random' and 'uncontrolled'—nevertheless, they were in fact exceedingly complex. Somewhere within the system there was a highly sophisticated computer which, given certain basic pieces of information, such as the time of day, the state of the weather, and the direction in which its owner-operator was heading, could calculate within seconds the number of trees, parked cars and various items of street furniture likely to be encountered en route. Armed with this information, the section which dealt with quantity control then dispensed measured doses with laboratory-like precision according to the total litreage available, the number of objects and their relative importance to each other.

The one thing Pommes Frites' system lacked was

any kind of early-warning system for the benefit of others. Short of lying in wait for him behind a tree, carrying out Durelle's request would not be easy.

Reflecting that even Sherlock Holmes might have admitted to being temporarily baffled by the problem, Monsieur Pamplemousse attempted to extract a crumb of comfort from the laden breakfast tray beside his bed.

Holmes had often begun his cases over breakfast. *The Hound of the Baskervilles* was a good example; breakfast consumed straight after an early-morning pipe filled with the previous day's dottle dried on the study mantelpiece. He must have had a constitution of iron.

Strange, the English predilection for a hearty breakfast. Perhaps it had to do with the uncertain climate. Boiled eggs, served in strange pottery containers, often shaped like hollowed-out human heads which grinned at you across the table. Knowing exactly when the eggs would be done to perfection was a mysterious art which was handed down and could not be described accurately in any cook book.

He wondered if a call from the Director would have been permitted to break the morning ritual at number 221B Baker Street. Mrs. Hudson would not have been pleased to see her efforts grow cold. Nothing, not even the sight of a newly severed digit in *The Adventure of the Engineer's Thumb* was ever allowed to put Holmes off his breakfast.

Monsieur Pamplemousse eyed the remains of his *brioche*. It looked most unappetising. Disappointing to start with, now that it had grown cold it was even less enticing. Perhaps it was yet another of Jean-Claude's skills which had not been passed on. Then, again, perhaps he was already conditioned to not expecting things exactly right; his expectations were now tempered by inside knowledge and the early-morning call from his office.

Crumbling the remains of the cake between thumb and forefinger, he debated his priorities; whether to attend to Pommes Frites or continue with his telephone calls. He decided on the latter. The longer he left Pommes Frites the stronger would be the call of nature once he surfaced.

The first number he dialled was engaged, the second was a garage in Evian. He apologised and tried the third number. It was a *cancoillotte* producer in a village higher up the mountains. *Cancoillotte,* made with well-rotted *Metton* cheese warmed over a low heat along with salt water and butter, was a speciality of the area. It was then melted again with white wine and garlic to be served as a fondue on toast or over potatoes. Just the thing after a ski run on a cold winter's day. The thought almost made him feel hungry again.

The fourth number was a flower shop in Evian. Something about the voice at the other end made him decide to try his luck.

'I am telephoning on behalf of Monsieur Parfait. Monsieur Jean-Claude Parfait. There is some confusion about an order.'

The girl sounded puzzled. There was the sound of rustling paper as if she was looking through an order book. 'Do you know when it was made? There is no record. Monsieur Jean-Claude usually calls in on his way back from market. Was it to do with the restaurant? Monsieur Albert always deals with that later in the day. He should be in any moment. I haven't seen Monsieur Jean-Claude for two days . . .'

'I'm sorry. I think I had better check.' Monsieur Pamplemousse made his excuses and hung up. Perhaps his remarks to the Director, made more in his own defence on the spur of the moment than for any other reason, were not so wide of the mark after all. It could still be a case of *cherchez la femme*. Jean-Claude would hardly be buying flowers for himself.

The sixth number was a ski club near Morzine.

He tried the first number again. This time he got the ringing tone. He counted over twenty rings and then a girl's voice answered. *'Bonjour. Vous voulez parler à qui?'* She sounded breathless. The words were French but the accent was foreign. He guessed it was English; the pitch went down at the end rather than up. Again, instinct told him to prolong the conversation. He plucked a name out of the air.

'Monsieur Duval, *s'il vous plaît.*'

*'Pardon?'*

He repeated the name. 'Monsieur Duval. Monsieur Henri Duval.'

The reply, when it came, was halting and confused, as if the speaker was suddenly out of her depth, struggling in heavy water. He decided to put her out of her misery.

*'Parlez-vous anglais?'*

'Yes. I mean . . . *oui.*' The relief was evident in the way the words came pouring out. 'I don't know anyone by that name. I think you'd better try the other number. This is the communal phone—the one for the pupils. I just happened to be passing.'

While he was listening, Monsieur Pamplemousse removed his pen from an inner pocket and twisted the barrel. 'Do you have the other number? I am afraid I have mislaid it.'

While he was writing there was a stirring from the confines of the wheelbarrow. It was followed by a loud yawn and a smacking of lips. Pommes Frites was showing signs of life at long last.

'And who shall I be speaking to?'

'You'll probably get Madame Schmidt herself. I saw her go towards her room as I was coming up the stairs.'

Thanking the girl for her trouble, he replaced the receiver and then almost immediately regretted his haste. Having established some kind of rapport he should have taken matters a stage further and found out where she was speaking from. The code was from an outside area. He checked with a list in a folder beside his bed. It was somewhere higher up the mountains near Morzine. It was obviously an educational establishment of some kind.

Monsieur Pamplemousse gazed thoughtfully at the telephone for a moment or two, then picked up the receiver and dialled the number the girl had given him.

This time the call was answered almost immediately.

'Institut des Beaux Arbres. Madame Schmidt speaking. Can I help you?'

He decided to take the bull by the horns. '*Bonjour, Madame*. I hope you can. Forgive my troubling you at this early hour, but I am in the area and I am making some enquiries. I am told that it is possible you have some vacancies.'

'The term has already started, *Monsieur*.' The voice sounded hesitant. 'We like our pupils to be here from the beginning, otherwise it sometimes creates difficulties. The school year begins in September.'

'No matter. There is no great urgency. It is a question of planning for the future. I am staying at Les Cinq Parfaits and while I am here I hope to see as many establishments as I can.'

'*Monsieur* should have an easy task then. As far as I know we are the only school in the area. They are nearly all on the Swiss side of the lake.'

'In that case perhaps it would be as well if I came to see you as soon as possible.'

'You have our brochure?'

'I am speaking on behalf of a friend. He is abroad at present and unable to carry out the investigation himself. I promised I would do my best.'

'He is French? Most of our clients are from overseas. Learning the language is an integral part of the course. A French student would find the going very slow.'

'No, *Madame*. He is English. That is also part of the problem and why I am here.'

'I understand, *Monsieur*.' The voice was perceptibly friendlier. 'The second half of this week will be a little difficult . . .'

'How about this afternoon?' Monsieur Pamplemousse assumed his most ingratiating manner. 'I realise it is very short notice, but my friend spoke most highly of your establishment, and with three children to plan for . . .'

This time there was a distinct thaw. 'Let me see . . . I have another appointment at four. Shall we say two thirty? That will allow plenty of time for you to see around the school and to observe our pupils at work.'

'Thank you, *Madame*. I will be with you at two thirty. *A bientôt*.'

'*Au revoir, Monsieur*.'

Pommes Frites looked at him enquiringly as he replaced the receiver. While his master had been engaged on the telephone he'd been taking stock of the situation, absorbing his new surroundings, weighing up the scene as best he could, given the fact that his brain was still far from functioning on all of its many cylinders. Not for nothing had he accompanied Monsieur Pamplemousse on his travels up and down the autoroutes and byways of France, sharing his thoughts at the wheel, his many meals, the passenger seat of his 2CV, and more often than not his hotel room—even his very bed. Over the years he'd become adept at reading his master's mind. Lack of vocabulary, at least on a scale which would have met the minimum requirements laid down by the Minister of Education for the schools of France, did not prevent him getting the gist of conversations or sensing which way the wind was blowing. Rather the reverse. The ability to recognise certain key words often gave him the edge in that it allowed him to go straight to the heart of matters at a time when others more skilled in their use would have been diverted. Instinct told Pommes Frites that something was going on.

However, coming up with the right answer was one thing. Co-ordinating the rest of his body to follow suit was another matter entirely. He tried shifting his position and then hurriedly froze as the surface beneath him rocked in a most unseemly manner and his stomach rebelled accordingly.

The plain fact was, Pommes Frites still felt distinctly out of sorts. Had he been given to writing to the newpapers on topics of current interest, he would have happily spent the rest of the morning lying in the wheelbarrow composing a very bitter letter indeed to the local *journal* on the subject of hotels who denied canine guests access to their dining-room and then left their waste-bins not only unattended but full to overflowing. It was simply asking for trouble. Religion was not one of Pommes Frites' strong subjects, but had he been cognisant of the temptations suffered by Adam in the Garden of Eden, he could have drawn some pretty pointed parallels. Nor would he have sought anonymity by signing himself 'Disgusted, Evian'; he would have come right out with it and given his full name and address. Whether the local *journal* would have risked incurring the wrath of Les Cinq Parfaits by printing it was purely a matter of conjecture; an editorial decision was unlikely to be put to the test. Les Cinq Parfaits was one of the area's major sources of income, a source whose ripples spread far and wide, giving support to innumerable diverse activities and industries, from mushroom-growers to helicopter pilots and the mechanics who serviced their machines, from wine-growers to owners of motor-launches, from chambermaids and dairy farmers to fruit-growers and butchers and suppliers of chlorine for swimming pools. Advertising revenue would have slumped and circulation figures been put in jeopardy.

However, it summed up the kind of mood Pommes Frites was in as he rested his head on the side of the barrow and watched his master busy himself over a matter that was clearly causing him a certain amount of serious thought and which involved emptying the contents of a small leather suitcase on to his bed.

The sight of the suitcase confirmed Pommes Frites' suspicions. Something was very definitely 'going on'.

Designed at the turn of the century by *Le Guide*'s

founder, Hippolyte Duval, for use by Inspectors at a time when emergencies of one sort or another were commonplace, it had been carefully added to and improved upon over the years until it had reached a point where practically any eventuality was catered for; even, reflected Monsieur Pamplemousse as he removed the tray of photographic equipment and exposed a lower one containing a selection of culinary items, eventualities which would surely have been undreamed of by the founder or any of his various successors.

Pommes Frites never ceased to be amazed by the contents of Monsieur Pamplemousse's suitcase, but amazement gave way to incredulity as he watched his master take out what looked like a very ordinary flat metal disc. Then, with one flick of his wrist, he changed it into a totally different shape—a shape not unlike a giant version of the ice-cream containers he was sometimes allowed to share, the ones which tasted of biscuit. Had his master produced a string of flags of all nations from his left ear, Pommes Frites could not have been more taken aback, and for the moment at least it took his mind off his own problems.

Nor did his master show signs of resting on his laurels. Having performed one trick to his obvious satisfaction, he looked around the room for another, peering into the bathroom, opening cupboard doors, until suddenly his gaze alighted on a large, empty bottle standing on top of the refrigerator.

Giving a grunt of satisfaction, Monsieur Pamplemousse slipped the cone-shaped article into the neck of the bottle, held both up to the light, then turned to face Pommes Frites, uttering as he did so the words, *'Une promenade?'*

Although simple in content and perhaps not in the same class as such immortal phrases as 'Kiss me, Hardy', or 'Not tonight, Josephine', they were, nevertheless, words which would have caused a keen student of such matters to prick up his ears and reach for a notebook, aware that he was privileged to be present at one of those moments destined to become in its own small way one of historical importance.

Blissfully unaware of either the importance of the occasion or the leading part he was about to play, Pommes Frites climbed out of the wheelbarrow and made his way unsteadily towards the door.

Even in his present comatose state he could tell the difference between a suggestion and a command. His early training with the Paris Sûreté stood him in good stead. Suggestions offered a freedom of choice. Commands were meant to be obeyed without question.

Conscious only that duty called, Pommes Frites followed his master out of the side door and into the gardens of Les Cinq Parfaits.

It was some while before they returned to the room and by then both were in sombre mood, each busy with his own thoughts and studiously avoiding the other's gaze.

The telephone was ringing, and while Pommes Frites lay down on a rug by the window, Monsieur Pamplemousse placed the bottle and funnel carefully on the table beside his bed and picked up the receiver. It was a call from Paris.

'Pamplemousse, what *is* going on? It was my intention to leave you to your own devices, but I have been receiving disturbing reports, reports I can scarcely credit. Reports of bestial happenings in the bushes outside the dining-room. There have been complaints from the guests. Some of them were so put off their lunch they demanded their money back. I would like to think that it was a case of mistaken identity, but I fear the description of both participants tallies. I demand an explanation.'

Monsieur Pamplemousse took a deep breath. There were times in his conversations with the Director when it was possible, by the lowering of suitable shutters, to divert the other's voice along the shortest possible route leading to an exit through the opposite ear, but patently it was not one of those occasions. Patently it was an occasion when tops needed to be blown, his authority asserted and parameters established once and for all.

He spoke at length, choosing his words with care; words which were both rounded and yet at the same time pointed. Explicit words which established his feelings with the utmost clarity and precision. Words which left no room for doubt. When he had finished he sat down on the bed and mopped his brow, waiting for the storm to break. Pommes Frites gazed at his master with renewed respect, aware that a stand had been made.

There was a long pause. 'Forgive me, Aristide.' The Director sounded genuinely contrite. 'I am under considerable pressure at this end, you understand. You are in the battle area, subject to bombardment by long-range missiles, but I am also under fire. Weapons are being held to my head. I have hardly slept all night.'

'*Pardon, Monsieur,*' Monsieur Pamplemousse broke in before the Director got too far with his emotional flights of fancy; once started there was often no stopping him. 'With respect, I must be allowed to do things in my own way and at my own pace. I have, I believe, already made considerable progress. Now there are leads to be followed; there is information to be tabulated and considered. However, it appears that there are others staying at Les Cinq Parfaits who know as much about what is going on as I do—possibly more—and who seem to be aware of my every movement. Not only aware,' he added with some heat, 'but only too anxious to report on them with all possible speed. Let these others do the dirty work.'

'That is not possible, Aristide. I cannot tell you why, but take my word for it, that is not possible. There are, as I said at the very beginning, wheels within wheels. Who knows what is what, or, indeed, who is who? If I were to tell you about some of the machinations which have reached my ears over the last two days you would scarcely credit them.'

Monsieur Pamplemousse rested the receiver under his chin and picked up the bottle containing Pommes Frites' sample. He held it up to the light. Château Pommes Frites. A direct comparison with the real thing would rank it immediately as from a poor year; there was a distinct orange tinge. Perhaps a '63? The year of a hard winter followed by a dismal summer, giving rise to poor flowering conditions. But that was only by direct comparison. On its own it would pass muster.

If his chief did but know it, he was preaching to the converted. Monsieur Pamplemousse was only too well aware of things that went on behind the scenes. Lack of communication. Empire building. Parkinson's Law, which rules that the appointment of two assistants instead of one meant that jobs could be divided up in such a way that no one person knew enough to become a potential threat to those above. Inter-departmental rivalry. Jockeying for power. Corridors which led nowhere except to closed doors. He'd come across many of those in his time. Blank faces. Denials of the very existence of things one knew only too well existed. Sometimes he wondered how governments functioned at all.

Wondering uneasily if he himself was some kind of pawn in the present game, he reached idly for the cork. It was still lying alongside the ice-bucket where it had been left the night before. Dried out by the warmth of the room, it went back into the neck of the bottle easily enough, needing only a slight tap with the ball of his hand to drive it fully home. There was only the smallest of holes to show where it had been penetrated by the corkscrew.

He held the bottle up to the light again and as he did so a wicked thought entered his mind. Durelle was no fool, but given that the original label was still intact, he might get away with it.

'Yes, chief, I am listening.' He felt decidedly more cheerful now. He couldn't wait to put his leg-pull into action. There would need to be a short note to accompany the bottle, of course. Something along the lines of: 'Pommes Frites now on the road to recovery. No need for further action. A small token of my appreciation. Hope you enjoy it. Aristide.'

It was true. Pommes Frites' eyes now had a decided sparkle. He was growing more alive by the minute. The walk and the consequent chase round the garden must have done him good.

Monsieur Pamplemousse slipped the lead foil over the neck and smoothed it into place. The wine waiter had done a good job. He must be a Capricorn like himself, as well as coming from the Auvergne; a perfectionist twice over. It looked as good as new.

'*Oui, Monsieur.* Rest assured, I will telephone the very moment there is anything to report. Possibly this evening.'

'And Aristide.' The Director hesitated, then swallowed hard. 'Forgive my impatience. It is always worse for those who stay behind. Things get magnified.'

'Of course, *Monsieur. Au revoir, Monsieur.*'

He opened the refrigerator and stood the bottle in the door-rack alongside its companion. With the capsule in place and in the artificially white light reflected from the interior it was almost indistinguishable from the real thing. If colour were the sole criterion, Pommes Frites would be in line for an award at the annual wine fair in Paris. There would have to be a P.S. to the message, otherwise Durelle would get suspicious. It was too good a gift. 'Have this one on the house. Madame Grante is paying.' That would appeal to his sense of humour too. Madame Grante in Accounts was notorious for watching every franc.

He glanced at his watch. There was hardly sufficient time for lunch in the restaurant. In any case he had no wish to run the gauntlet of those who had spotted their activities in the bushes, and Pommes Frites might not take kindly to eating by himself twice running. Perhaps a snack by the pool would be the answer. He'd seen a cold table laid out there. A little *charcuterie;* some *saucisses de Morteau et de Montbeliard*—cumin-flavoured—a speciality of the region. Some ham from Chamonix—dried in the crisp mountain air. A salad. Then some *Beaufort* or some *Comté;* perhaps a little of each. If they got a move on there might be time for some bilberry tart to follow—or some more raspberries; they wouldn't be around for very much longer.

If he was lucky they might have some sparkling wine from Seyssel—the most northern of the Rhône vineyards and the nearest thing to champagne. A glass or two would set him up for the rest of the day. He could accompany the rest of the meal with some flinty rosé d'Arbois. It would be light enough not to make him feel sleepy or impede his thought processes.

Pommes Frites rose and accompanied him to the door.

Outside, Monsieur Pamplemousse reversed the card on the handle, changing the sign from one showing a girl in a white dress and old-fashioned bonnet asleep under a walnut tree to one of her hard at work with a feather duster. Halfway along the corridor there was a large trolley laden with sheets and towels, bottles of Evian and packets of soap and perfume. From an open doorway he heard the murmur of voices and some suppressed giggles. The room maids must be getting near.

He glanced down at Pommes Frites as they set off. Pommes Frites looked up and wagged his tail. It was a good sign. One good sign, followed almost immediately by a second, for he licked his lips, and if Pommes Frites was licking his lips it could mean only one thing: life was returning to normal.

# 5

## L'INSTITUT DES BEAUX ARBRES

IT TOOK MONSIEUR PAMPLEMOUSSE RATHER longer than he'd planned to get within striking distance of the Institut des Beaux Arbres, and even longer to find the entrance, which was half-hidden behind a clump of fir trees.

Reflecting that the Institut was well-named (most of the *arbres* were not only *beaux,* they were *très grands* as well, and badly needed thinning), he pulled in alongside some large wrought-iron gates standing in splendid isolation within a carved stone archway and climbing out of the car he applied his thumb to a bell-push. A disembodied voice emerged from a small grille above the button. He gave his name and almost immediately there was a buzz from the direction of the gate itself as an electric bolt-retainer slid open. There was a click and the loudspeaker was silent, cutting off the apologies he had been about to make for being late. He glanced at his watch. It was almost three o'clock.

Lunch had been a protracted affair. Word must have got around about his extravagance the previous evening, for a second assistant *sommelier* hovered about his table like a solicitous butterfly, the *carte des vins* already open at what he clearly considered to be an appropriately expensive page. At the waiter's suggestion he had weakened and succumbed to a whole bottle of Pouilly-Fumé instead of the half-bottle of rosé he'd had in mind; a Baron de 'L' '82 from the estate of the Ladoucette family in Pouilly-sur-Loire. Totally delicious, it prompted an entry in his notebook as a reminder to repeat the experience at the earliest opportunity—God, Monsieur le Directeur and Madame Grante in Accounts permitting.

The combination of the wine, food from a cold table positively groaning with temptations, coupled with a somewhat protracted but undeniably thorough survey of such *doudounes* as were on public display around the pool that day, left him in the end with the bare minimum of time to rush back to his room, grab the bottle containing Pommes Frites' sample from the door of the fridge and his Leica from the case, before making an equally wild dash for Evian and the nearest *gare*. He'd been in and out before the maid, busy replenishing the stocks of perfume and unguents in the bathroom, even realised what was happening.

The journey to Evian had been slow; the normally quiet lakeside road busier than usual. Lausanne, on the far side of Lac Léman, was shrouded in autumn mist, the hills beyond barely visible. In one village an unlikely-looking, life-sized painted cut-out of a cow eyed him dolefully as he waited his turn in the traffic which had piled up behind a delivery van parked outside an *épicerie*. It looked decidedly less happy than its real-life counterparts in the fields he had passed on the way down, and he could hardly blame it.

After Evian he headed for the D22 and then turned left in the direction of the mountains, taking a road which grew steadily more narrow and winding. Wooden chalets with tightly shuttered windows dotted the hillside. Alongside them stood piles of neatly sawn logs ready for the coming winter. They were all so similar and so like toy musical-boxes that it wouldn't have been surprising to see a giant key on the outside of each one, to wind them up again in the spring.

Gradually the chalets retreated, to be replaced by isolated farms; the road became steeper, the drop more sheer, making it difficult to overtake anything in front—even the occasional cyclists enjoying a last seasonal fling as they pedalled their way laboriously uphill with lowered heads and bulging thighs. Why was it they always seemed to be going uphill rather than down? It looked very painful and unpleasurable, although he had done exactly the same thing when he'd been their age. There was hardly a hill in the Auvergne he hadn't tackled in his youth, and he must have enjoyed it at the time.

Having got well and truly stuck behind a laborious sand-carrying *camion,* Monsieur Pamplemousse took the opportunity to run through in his mind the reasons for making the journey at all. It was really little more than the following up of a hunch; a feeling he couldn't have put into words. But that was how it was; how it had always been. How many times in the past had he not set off on a journey with as little to go on? That was what it was all about. You started with a problem. Then you took all the available facts and you placed them in some kind of order. Perhaps, if the worst came to the worst you put them all into a hat and gave them a good shake. Then you played a hunch.

Holmes would have done the same. Except, of course, he would have carried it through with total conviction and from the comfort of his lodging house. He tried to picture what Holmes might have told Watson before despatching him up the mountainside in a pony and trap.

First, there was the fact that Jean-Claude's disappearance had not been premeditated, of that he was sure. Had it been, he would have taken more with him. All his toiletries seemed to be intact. There was no marked absence of clothes or suitcases.

Secondly, he was well-known in the area. If he had caught a train or an *autobus* anywhere someone would have seen him, assuming Albert Parfait was telling the truth—and apart from a disquieting feeling that for some reason best known to himself he wasn't being entirely frank, he couldn't for the moment see any reason why he should be lying. Jean-Claude's car was still at Les Cinq Parfaits—that was a puzzle. If anything, it pointed to his not having gone very far, or to his having gone with someone else.

Thirdly, there was the strange encounter in the wood. Fourthly, there was the collection of words he'd come across under Jean-Claude's blotter. How or why they fitted into the overall picture he hadn't the remotest idea. That the words formed a blackmail note of some kind was obvious, but how it related to Jean-Claude's disappearance was another matter.

Lastly, there was the picture of the girl he was carrying in his pocket along with the list of telephone numbers. That the girl was the reason for Jean-Claude's visits to the flower shop he had no doubt; that she was a pupil of the Institut des Beaux Arbres seemed more than likely. She was about the right age. She was English. It was the only school in the area.

Hairpin bends, the nearside edge protected by low stone walls or steel safety-barricades—some bent and twisted where previous drivers had tried to negotiate the corners too fast, caused the lorry in front to slow down almost to walking pace. Frustrated, he stopped in a lay-by and consulted his map. The view down to the valley on his right was breathtaking. In a field just below him an old woman was bent double over a mound of freshly dug potatoes. Nearby a man was picking fruit from a tree. The sound of what seemed like a thousand bells, all tuned to a different pitch, floated up from neatly parcelled areas of pastureland as cows and sheep dipped their heads to munch the rich grass. Old white porcelain baths filled with water for the cattle dotted the landscape, bequeathed by owners who had become affluent and exchanged them in the name of progress for brightly coloured suites made of plastic or fibreglass.

As he set off in the car again he fell to wondering if Albert knew of the girl's existence. If so, did he approve? Apart from the question of age, he saw no outward reason for disapproval. If he'd had a son of his own, he would have been more than happy. Come to think of it, if the girl had been his daughter he would have felt equally happy. Or would he? Jean-Claude would be something of a catch. Anyone who married him would have to be fairly special; the life was not an easy one. Nor would Albert wish to see his son diverted from his chosen path—or, more to the point, the one that he had chosen for him. Already his absence had caused unrest, but that was hardly a reason for family jiggery-pokery. Besides, a girl who had been given the added benefit of a spell at a finishing school, versed in the social graces, ought to be ideal.

He tried to picture her again, sitting in the restaurant, an altogether more vulnerable figure than the one in the photograph. Since she had been alone and clearly worried, she was probably as much in the dark as he was. He found himself wanting to help her if it was at all possible.

He began toying with the idea of asking Madame Schmidt outright if he could see the girl. She could hardly refuse. On the other hand, he had probably made it impossible; by a chance word he had burned his boats. Madame Schmidt would hardly believe him now if he came up with a story about being a friend of the family who happened to be in the area.

He saw the sign marking the turn-off for the Institut a moment too late. Reversing the 2CV wasn't easy, especially as Pommes Frites was beginning to show signs of what American astronauts in their quaint jargon called 'stomach awareness', and insisted on sitting bolt upright with a pained expression on his face, looking neither to the right nor to the left, as if the problem was not of his making—which, in fairness, it wasn't.

The road leading up to the school was narrower

still. Unusually, Michelin seemed to have ignored its existence, eschewing even the doubtful honour of awarding it a single dotted black line on their map of the area. The only sign, just before the entrance, had been one warning of danger from falling rock.

He opened the gates, drove through, then stopped to get out and close them again. The bolt clicked home. Madame Schmidt obviously took good care of her pupils. To one side there was a passing place large enough to accommodate a whole fleet of limousines. From the gate the road dropped down again towards a hidden valley and then, a few hundred metres further on, he encountered a junction with a bevy of signs pointing in different directions: to the left, the staff quarters and the delivery area; straight on to the recreation area, students' chalets and visitors' carpark. The main building lay to the right.

There were three other cars parked outside the house: a black Mercedes 220 with a Swiss registration, and two Peugeot 505s—one with a local registration and the other bearing a Paris 75 on its number-plate. The one from Paris looked as if it had recently been driven through a heavy rainstorm; the sides were flecked with mud almost to window-height and there were clear patches on the windscreen where the wipers had been used. Whoever had been at the wheel had been in a hurry.

Madame Schmidt was waiting at the door to greet him. She looked as if she were used to people being late. His apologies were brushed aside as of no great consequence.

Pommes Frites didn't look at all put out at being left in the car; rather the reverse. He assumed his 'aloof from it all, see you when I see you' expression

93

as he curled up in the front seat to await further instructions. Nevertheless, as the door to the Institut des Beaux Arbres closed behind his master he sat up and automatically registered a quick movement behind one of the windows, the falling into place of a curtain. Having stored the information in the back of his mind in case it was ever needed, he closed his eyes and went to sleep again.

Inside the house, Monsieur Pamplemousse was also busily committing various items to memory. Not only the restrained but undoubted luxury of the furnishings and the depth of the carpeting, but also Madame Schmidt herself. Madame Schmidt wasn't quite as he'd expected her to be and it was hard to say exactly why. He always felt ill at ease with members of the teaching profession; they tended to talk in statements or to ask questions which demanded answers. But it wasn't just that. Following her across the hall he sensed a contradiction in styles. On the telephone she had sounded nervous and abrupt, whereas listening to her now she seemed much more to be mistress of the situation. Perhaps it was simply a case of being on her home ground, but somehow he felt it was more than that.

He guessed she must be in her middle sixties. It was hard to tell with some people, particularly those who were able to keep up appearances. Elderly and benign, she could have been everyone's 'Tante Marie', had her grey hair not been quite so impeccably coiffeured, her skin so smooth and wrinkle-free. She defied cursory cataloguing. Her silk blouse reflected Paris chic rather than local tastes, which veered towards spa-town sensible. Heavy jewellery adorned fingers that were long and thin and beautifully manicured. He caught a whiff of expensive perfume as she paused to open the door to her study. Fees at the Institut des Beaux Arbres must either be considerable to keep her in the style to which she was clearly accustomed, or she had independent means.

Motioning him towards an armchair in the centre of the room, she handed him a folder before seating herself behind a desk near the window with her back to the light, making a steeple with her hands. He suddenly felt as though he were back at school, about to be grilled regarding a broken window in the greenhouse.

'Your friend will find all he needs to know inside the folder—the practical details, that is. Most of it is contained in the brochure; the rest are application forms, details of the various courses we have to offer, term times, fees and so forth. Also items like insurance and accident indemnity forms.'

'You seem to have thought of everything,' he murmured.

Madame Schmidt inclined her head. 'We have been established for over thirty years.'

Her accent, although hard to fault, was again hard to place. It was almost too impeccable. He had a feeling that she wasn't French born. It was a feeling that was confirmed almost before he had time to open the folder.

'I was born in England. My husband is German-speaking Swiss. Between us we are able to supervise the teaching of most European languages. The majority of our pupils have English as their first language when they arrive. In fact many of them *are* English.'

Monsieur Pamplemousse glanced through the folder

and then turned to the brochure. Wide-angle lenses did the Institut des Beaux Arbres more than justice; the house itself certainly looked much grander than in reality. But if the photographs gave a false impression, the curriculum more than made up for the deception. He ran his eyes down the list. *Cuisine—nouvelle* and *haute* (with the opportunity of learning over one hundred and fifty new recipes per term); the mind boggled. Domestic science included engagement and control of domestic staff, ironing, washing-up (by hand and machine)—presumably for those who couldn't afford servants—and car maintenance (overalls supplied). Protocol covered *savoir-vivre*, the art of conversation and the theory and practice of baptisms and children's parties—perhaps for those who hadn't learned to say no in enough languages during the first part of their course. Elegance and deportment were catered for as well as flower arrangement (according to season). There were classes on child psychology, typing, bridge, art and clay modelling. The list seemed endless. He thought of Jean-Claude.

'Any girl who masters all these things will be much sought after.'

'Some of our pupils have married into the best families of Europe,' said Madame Schmidt complacently. 'They are, indeed, much sought after.'

Discarding a leaflet on supplementary cultural trips which included visits to a watch factory in Geneva and the kitchen of a restaurant near Lausanne (no doubt it would be Girardet), Monsieur Pamplemousse picked up another pamphlet dealing with the various sporting facilities available: riding, windsurfing, water-skiing, sailing, climbing, golf, ice-skating, skiing. He suddenly stiffened on turning the page as a familiar picture swam into view: a group of male skiers. He'd last seen it in his room at the hotel when it had fallen out of the envelope belonging to Jean-Claude. Under it was the caption '*Nos professeurs de ski*'.

'You have a permanent staff of ski instructors?' He tried to make the question sound as casual as possible.

'Naturally. In the summer they do other things, of course. But we like to preserve continuity.' Madame Schmidt regarded him across the top of her desk. 'Perhaps, before we set out on a brief tour of the school, *Monsieur* would like to fill in the registration form giving details of your friend's children. You realise there is almost always a long waiting-list so it is necessary that we have some form of selection. It may take time.'

The implication that his friend's children might not measure up to the Institut des Beaux Arbres' requirements was not lost on Monsieur Pamplemousse. Perhaps if he'd been driving something more exotic than a *deux chevaux* the question would not have arisen.

'I think you will find their background is impeccable. References of the highest order will be made available. For the time being, I am not allowed to reveal the name of my friend—for diplomatic reasons, you understand . . .' A barely perceptible reshaping of the steeple warned him that for some reason he had said the wrong thing. 'I mean, of course, in the sense that it would not be right for me to pre-empt any decision on his part without prior consultation.' Madame Schmidt visibly relaxed.

'You say he has *three* daughters? If you care to fill in their Christian names and a few brief details regarding their ages and previous schooling . . . the colour of their hair . . . any special interests . . .'

97

Monsieur Pamplemousse's heart sank as he felt for his pen. His knowledge of the English educational system was hazy in the extreme, other than the fact that public schools were anything but that implied by the name. The perfidious Albions were past masters at the art of calling a spade by anything rather than its proper name. They had 'stands' for sitting down, and places called 'downs' that were really ups. They had conquered half the world that way before opting out and leaving it in a state of confusion.

Names like Eton and Harrow sprang to mind, but he had a feeling that they were for boys only; it was part of the English habit to segregate the sexes at an early age, a habit that gave rise to problems later on. A colleague had once had a bizarre encounter in Boulogne with a party of girls from a school on the Channel coast; he still talked about it, releasing tantalising details in the canteen from time to time. It was worth a try.

'It is on the south coast of England. Somewhere near Brighton. Where the rock comes from.' That had been part of the story. It had had them all on the edge of their chairs.

'Roedean?' Madame Schmidt sounded impressed.

'Roedean.' He put pen to paper. It was not an easy word to spell. Worse than that place near London. The one they spelt like 'rough' and pronounced like 'cow'. The language was full of pitfalls. He crossed out the first attempt and tried again. It looked even less likely and he felt glad he wasn't applying for a place.

'They are all three at Roedean?'

'My friend is very wealthy.' He racked his brains for some suitable names. It was dreadful how the mind went completely blank at such times. Thinking up names in one's own tongue was bad enough, but

English! There had been the landlady's daughter in Torquay where he'd stayed during his visit to England. She'd taught him a lot more than differences in the language. *Entente* between the two countries had never been more *cordiale*. She'd had a friend who'd also been impressively advanced for her years. He decided to try his luck again.

'I don't recall our ever having had an Ada here before,' said Madame Schmidt with a distinct lack of enthusiasm. 'Or a Reet.'

'Simple names are often the best,' said Monsieur Pamplemousse, conscious that his stock was sinking again. 'I have read that in England they are coming back into favour. It has to do with the Royal Family,' he added vaguely.

The thought triggered off another. 'It is, however, Diana who is the prime concern. The other two have a few years to go yet. Diana is barely eighteen and her father is a little worried about her. She is a lovely girl in every way, but I'm afraid her academic qualifications leave a lot to be desired. It is her parents' wish that she continue with her education for a few more years. There are so many temptations for a girl these days, especially those who have the misfortune to look older than they are. Drink . . . drugs . . . sex . . . it is a difficult age.

'Not,' he continued, warming to his subject, 'that she has experienced any of these things . . . yet. They lead a sheltered life at Roedean.'

'She sounds,' said Madame Schmidt thoughtfully, 'just the kind of girl we like to have at the Institut des Beaux Arbres. Do you have a photograph?'

'A photograph?' Carried away by enthusiasm for his subject, emboldened by the after-effects of the

wine he'd consumed at lunch, Monsieur Pamplemousse found himself reaching for his wallet. 'But, of
course. I always carry one. She is, after all, my
god-daughter.'

Brandishing the photograph taken from Jean-
Claude's room, he handed it across the table and
then sat back to see what happened.

But if Monsieur Pamplemousse was expecting any
kind of reaction, he was disappointed. Madame
Schmidt held the photograph up to the light and
gazed at it intently for several long moments. 'A very
pretty girl,' she said, in much the same tone of voice
as she might have used to comment on one of her
pupil's flower arrangements. 'From all you have told
me I am sure we can give the application every
consideration.'

Rising to her feet she took the completed form
from Monsieur Pamplemousse and then led the way
out into the corridor. 'Perhaps you wouldn't mind
waiting here.' She motioned towards a chair. 'I shan't
keep you more than a moment. If I may, I will have
this photograph copied so that it can go with the
application. I do think it's so useful to have a clear
picture of whoever one is dealing with, don't you?'

Without waiting for a reply, she entered a room on
the opposite side of the corridor and closed the door
firmly behind her. Almost immediately there came a
murmur of voices. First Madame Schmidt's, then
male voices. It sounded as though there were at least
two others in the room, possibly three. Monsieur
Pamplemousse took the opportunity to remove the
lens cap from his camera and check that the expo-
sure system was in the correct mode. He cocked the
shutter and then listened outside the door for a mo-

ment. The voices were much too low to make any sense out of what was being said, but from the tone of the conversation it sounded as though it might go on for a few more minutes at least.

He glanced around. There were three other doors, two further along the corridor, one on either side, and another at the far end. Larger than the others, the third one had a red cross painted on the outside and he guessed it must be the Sanatorium.

He decided to seize the opportunity to do some exploring. If he met anyone he could always say he was looking for a toilet.

The first door opened into an office. It was empty. A typewriter, its cover neatly in place, sat on an otherwise clear desk near the window. In the far corner was a copying machine. He wondered if the Institut ran to two such machines or whether the photograph had been used as an excuse. The second room turned out to be a library of sorts. It was also empty. Both rooms were dark and neither worth wasting any film on.

The door to the Sanatorium was locked. As he tried the handle he thought he detected a hurried movement on the other side. On an impulse he half-raised his camera, waist-high, finger on the shutter release button, but no one materialised. Just as he was about to try the handle for a second time he heard the sound of a door being closed somewhere behind him. He pressed the button as he turned. If Madame Schmidt registered the fact she showed no sign other than by a quick glance at the camera.

'I think you will find that everything of interest has already been photographed for the brochure, *Monsieur* . . . ?'

You don't know my name, thought Monsieur Pamplemousse, because I didn't give it to you. He decided there was nothing to be gained by concocting a false one. He'd had enough of inventing names for one day. Madame Schmidt would find out soon enough if she really wanted to know.

'Pamplemousse.' He wound the film on. 'Photography is a hobby of mine. I'm afraid I am a compulsive picture-taker. But as you say, it is good to have a clear picture of whoever one is dealing with.'

His reward was an enigmatic smile which was hard to classify; wintry Mona Lisa, perhaps? Madame Schmidt looked pointedly at her watch and then turned to lead the way in the opposite direction.

'If you will forgive me, I think we should begin our tour. There are many things to show you and I have another appointment at four.'

Monsieur Pamplemousse stood his ground. 'It is not possible to see the Sanatorium while I am here? It was one of the areas my friend was particularly anxious I should report on. Diana is a little delicate and when one's child is away from home in a foreign country . . .'

'I'm afraid it is occupied at the moment. A serious skiing accident. The patient must not be disturbed.'

'Is it not a little early for a skiing accident?' persisted Monsieur Pamplemousse.

'Early ones are the very worst.' Madame Schmidt's smile took on another layer of frost. 'People try to run before they can walk. They are over-confident. It is always bad to be over-confident.'

Monsieur Pamplemousse gave up the struggle and followed her down the corridor. 'Do you have many such casualties?'

'All winter sports are dangerous,' said Madame Schmidt. She paused before opening another door. 'Those to do with the mountains most of all. To some the mountains mean white gold—they are a source of power and energy. To others they can mean death. Sadly, we have had our share of bad luck, but these things go in cycles. I think you will find that overall our record stands comparison with many other similar establishments. If people have been telling you otherwise then I suggest you do not listen to them. It does not do to listen to idle gossip.'

Monsieur Pamplemousse looked at her with mild surprise. His remark had been intended merely as a pleasantry, a bridge to get them from one talking point to another, nothing more. What was it the great English playwright, William Shakespeare, had said? 'The lady doth protest too much, methinks.'

'I will take you first to the lecture rooms.' Changing the subject abruptly, Madame Schmidt led the way across a small courtyard towards a more modern brick-built building. 'Here, the girls are taught secretarial work—shorthand and typing—needlework, painting, and various social activities. We also have our language laboratory. New girls spend a great deal of time there during the first few weeks. All our classes are conducted in French and some of them have a good deal of catching up to do. Diana has French?'

'Diana,' said Monsieur Pamplemousse non-committally, 'has a great many languages. Her parents are much travelled.' He followed Madame Schmidt down a long corridor peering at empty rooms through glass panels in the doors. 'Do you have many pupils at any one time?'

'It varies,' said Madame Schmidt, avoiding, as he

**103**

had, a direct answer. 'We pride ourselves on giving individual attention. Staff sometimes outnumber the pupils.' She stopped by a noticeboard and ran her finger down a chart. 'This afternoon, for example, many of the girls are making the most of the good weather enjoying a run with our Matron and gym mistress, Fräulein Brünnhilde. The rest are either doing revision in their own rooms or they are engaged in a cooking lesson.

'*Regardez!*' She paused by a door near the end of the corridor and looked through the panel. 'I think perhaps it will be as well if we do not disturb them. They are making a cake in honour of our patron's visit and they seem to have reached a delicate stage.'

Monsieur Pamplemousse focused his gaze on a small group of girls in white aprons struggling with an enormous jug of melted chocolate which they were endeavouring to pour over a castle-shaped edifice. Beyond them he could see a line of stoves and racks of kitchen equipment: saucepans and plates, knives and other paraphernalia. It all looked highly organised.

He glanced back at the group round the table, wondering if he might strike lucky and see the girl from the restaurant but she didn't appear to be there.

'It seems to be a very large cake,' he remarked. 'Large and rich.'

'Our patron has a very sweet tooth,' said Madame Schmidt. 'And an insatiable appetite.'

As she spoke they both heard the sound of a dog barking. Monsieur Pamplemousse pricked up his ears. To be more specific, it was the sound of Pommes Frites barking. He sounded cross about something, although not so much cross as put-out or bothered. His voice was distinctly *agitato*.

He turned away from the window. 'Perhaps I shouldn't keep you any longer,' he began. 'If you are busy . . .'

'As you wish, *Monsieur*.' It was hard to tell whether Madame Schmidt was pleased or otherwise. 'As I said earlier, you will find all you wish to know in the brochure. If you have any other questions you can always telephone. No doubt your friend will be in touch when he has had a chance to consider the matter?'

'No doubt.' As they crossed the courtyard again and approached the main building, the barking stopped. Each, for different reasons, noted the fact with relief.

Back inside the hall he paused by the front door. 'I wonder if I might have the photograph of my god-daughter back?'

'Of course. Forgive me. I had forgotten.' She seemed to have slipped back into her 'Tante Marie' role again. 'I won't keep you a moment.'

As Madame Schmidt disappeared from view Monsieur Pamplemousse stepped outside. Pommes Frites was standing on the passenger seat of the *deux chevaux* peering through the windscreen. He seemed pleased to see his master and as soon as the car door was open he leapt out and ran round the outside on a tour of inspection.

'*Qu'est-ce que c'est?*' Monsieur Pamplemousse followed on behind, but could see nothing. Perhaps someone had been having a quiet prowl while his back was turned. They would have had short shrift from Pommes Frites if they'd tried to look inside the car itself.

He glanced around the area. The Peugeot with the

Paris registration was no longer there. He focused the Leica and took a few pictures for luck; first the remaining cars, then the main building. He was about to frame up the entrance when Madame Schmidt appeared in the doorway holding his photograph. He caught her registering a moment of disapproval. '*Fromage*' rather than the Anglo-Saxon word 'cheese' formed on her lips.

Pommes Frites, clearly less than happy with the situation, climbed back into the car and sat waiting for his seat-belt to be fastened, making it absolutely clear that as far as he was concerned it was high time they left. Without being able to put his finger on a specific reason, Monsieur Pamplemousse had an uneasy feeling he could be right.

'You are journeying far, Monsieur Pappernick? To Paris, perhaps?'

'The name is Pamplemousse.' He slipped the photograph back into his wallet. 'No, we shall stay in the area for a little while longer. The weather is too good at present not to take advantage of it.'

'You are wise. I am told Paris is very wet.' Madame Schmidt held out her hand. '*Au revoir et bonne chance.*'

'*Au revoir, Madame.*' Monsieur Pamplemousse climbed in alongside Pommes Frites, fastened both seat-belts and closed the door. '*Et merci beaucoup.* I hope I haven't kept you.'

He swung the car round in a circle and changed up into second gear before beginning the long climb towards the main gate. He caught a final glimpse of Madame Schmidt in the driving mirror as she stood watching their progress from the doorway. Suddenly she was joined by someone else—a man, but the road curved sharply to the right and they both disappeared from view.

The gates at the top of the drive were open; perhaps left that way by the driver of the Peugeot. On the basis of never looking a gift horse in the mouth, he took advantage of his good fortune and breasted the top of the slope at speed, with the result that he came out through the other side of the archway rather faster than he had intended.

In retrospect, reliving the moment later that night, he realised fate must have taken a hand in the proceedings; either that or whichever guardian angel with culinary inclinations had been allocated the task of looking after employees of *Le Guide* that afternoon. Had he been travelling any faster he would almost certainly have crashed through the low retaining wall opposite and hurtled down into the valley below—a thought which didn't bear dwelling on; nor could he have avoided mowing down a group of girls in shorts and singlets who were about to turn in to the driveway, straight across his path.

In the event, the car slewed round, missed hitting both wall and runners by a hair's-breadth, rocked, then miraculously righted itself again and rushed onward. He was aware of a number of things happening almost simultaneously. Or rather, he was aware that certain things were *not* happening as they should. Although his right foot was almost pushing the brake pedal through the floor, it had no effect whatsoever. He could hear the sound of girls screaming, and out of the corner of his eye he could see Pommes Frites' seat-belt was being tested to its limit. Then there was a crash as they cannoned into the road sign a little way down the hill and at last came to an abrupt halt.

'*Merde!*' Monsieur Pamplemousse released both safety-belts and together with Pommes Frites climbed

107

out of the car and hurried round the front to view the extent of the damage. It was less than he'd feared; much less than the sound of the crash suggested. Not for nothing had Monsieur Boulanger kept his designers' sights firmly fixed on two of the main requirements he'd laid down—a long life and minimum repairs. The minuscule dent in the front bumper would have brought joy to their hearts, the dent on the offside wing confirmed their policy of separate and replaceable body parts. The road sign had fared much worse. It now stood at a drunken angle, looking as if it had failed to heed its own warning of danger from falling rocks.

'Monsieur . . . are you hurt? Such bravery . . . such panache . . . to drive straight into a *signalisation routière*, and without a moment of hesitation.'

A shadow fell across the bumper as Monsieur Pamplemousse bent down to examine it more closely. It was accompanied by the sound of a woman's voice, slightly out of breath.

He turned and looked up, irritated by the interruption. 'It was nothing. It was our good fortune that the sign happened to be there. Had it not been . . .' Monsieur Pamplemousse left the sentence unfinished, partly because there was no need to labour the point, but mostly because he found himself face to face with, indeed almost touching, two very good reasons why at that moment in time the sun's rays were blocked out. Rising and falling as their owner crouched beside him, they loomed into view like the distant peaks of le Dent d'Oche in the background far behind. A distinct feeling of déjà vu swept over him, and for a brief but disturbing second he was sorely tempted to reach up and attempt a renewal of his experience the night before by way of confirmation. But the moment passed. The sight of a group of girls standing a little way back watching his every movement made him think better of it. Instead, he rose to his feet and converted the movement into one of running his hand over his hair, much as he often did when he was caught about to commit some minor traffic misdemeanour.

The woman coloured slightly as she read his thoughts. '*Monsieur* is too modest. We might all have been killed. How can I ever thank you?'

Monsieur Pamplemousse hesitated. 'Perhaps, *Mademoiselle* . . .'

'*Fräulein* . . . Fräulein Brünnhilde. I am in charge of the physical well-being of the girls at the Institut.' She gestured in the direction of the waiting group. 'We were returning from a run. Normally the gates would have been closed. That is why it came as a surprise.'

Following the direction of her hand, Monsieur Pamplemousse's senses quickened yet again. There were perhaps a dozen or more girls and among them he spied the one he'd been looking for. She caught his eye and he thought he detected a faint glint of recognition, a momentary ray of hope. She looked tired and desperately unhappy.

Strengthened in his resolve, he decided to take the plunge. 'Perhaps, Fräulein Brünnhilde, if you really feel in my debt you would join me for dinner tonight? I am staying at Les Cinq Parfaits. It would give me great pleasure.'

'I think that would not be possible. I am also the Matron. Evenings are difficult. Besides, I do not own a car.'

It wasn't a total brush-off. He decided to try again.

'*Déjeuner*, then? We could have it by the pool?' It would be an opportunity to sample the Baron de 'L' again. It would be interesting to see what effect it had on his guest.

She hesitated. 'That, too, would be difficult. Perhaps . . . a picnic?'

'A picnic? Certainly. I will meet you here at twelve.' It was all too easy. Normally he would never have plucked up the courage. He wondered how many opportunities in life were let slip through lack of courage and simple communication.

'13.00 would be better.' She gave a nervous giggle. 'I shall need to play truant.' The words were imbued with a *soupçon* of wickedness. He wondered whether it was intentional or simply lack of command of the language.

'*D'accord*. Tomorrow then.'

'*Auf Wiedersehen!*'

As he waved goodbye, Monsieur Pamplemousse became aware of a restless stirring beside him. Pommes Frites was getting impatient.

Pommes Frites was right, of course, as he so often was. Time was of the essence. There were important matters to investigate. Things needed looking into, or rather under. As Fräulein Brünnhilde and her party disappeared through the gates, Monsieur Pamplemousse got down on his hands and knees and peered under the car. A brief glance confirmed his suspicions.

From a similar position on the other side of the body Pommes Frites gave what looked remarkably like a nod of agreement. He was not a particularly mechanically-minded dog; the intricacies of hydraulically operated braking-systems passed him by. In emergencies he much preferred his own tried and tested arrangement, that of digging two enormous front paws into whatever ground happened to be available at the time. Now the sight of an open pipe dangling beneath the chassis of the car only served to confirm him in his views. It also confirmed his feeling that someone was out to nobble his master, and if that were the case then he not only had a very good idea who was responsible, but when the deed had actually taken place.

# 6

## POMMES FRITES MAKES A DISCOVERY

MONSIEUR PAMPLEMOUSSE SEATED HIMSELF IN a chair of an open-air bar overlooking the port in Evian, unwrapped a piece of sugar, broke it in two, dropped the smaller of the two halves into a cup of *café noir*, then settled back in order to contemplate the world in general and his own immediate plans in particular.

The world in general consisted at that moment in time of a row of gulls staring back at him from a position of safety on the harbour wall, a small flotilla of sailing boats halfway across the lake towards Lausanne, two couples at nearby tables, some old-age pensioners waiting patiently for the arrival of a little rubber-tyred train which ran to and fro along the promenade, a few lorries on their way to Switzerland, and a sprinkling of late holiday-makers taking the morning air.

It was all very peaceful and ordered, reminding him that soon after his enforced early retirement from the Paris Sûreté, he'd once toyed with the idea of going there to live. All he'd wanted was to escape from it all. But Doucette, after one night of being kept awake by cowbells, had put her foot down and it had remained a pipe-dream. Doucette always woke at the first creak, or so she said, never the second. He'd consoled himself with the thought that for most people happiness lay in dreams of what might have been.

His own immediate plans were another matter and to some extent dependent on what fate and Fräulein Brünnhilde had in store. Of the two, he felt that fate could prove more reliable and predictable. Fräulein Brünnhilde had a slightly worrying gleam in her eye.

Alongside him stood two large plastic carrier-bags. One contained two bottles of Evian water, a bottle of red Mondeuse, and a long, heavy-duty cardboard postal tube. The other carrier-bag, with a second one inside it for safety's sake, bulged with goodies culled that morning from the *charcuteries, traiteurs* and *boulangeries* of Evian. *Saucisses de Morteau et de Montbéliard* rubbed shoulders with pork and cabbage *saucisses de chou, gâteau de foies blonds de volaille* pressed against smoked mountain ham sliced from the bone and sachets of thicker ham stuffed with fresh pork meat—*jambonnettes* the like of which he hadn't seen since he'd last visited Mère Montagne's shop in Lamastre, on the other side of the Rhône valley.

The central layer in the bag was made up of a large wedge of *Reblochon* and a generous helping of *Morbier* which he'd been unable to resist; two thin layers of cheese coated with charcoal on their opposing sides before being squeezed into a rich, cake-like ball out of which oozed a thin black line.

A crisp *baguette* poked up through the middle of the bag like an over-fat flagpole, surrounded by other delicacies from the same *boulangère; tarte aux myrtilles, galette de goumeau*—*brioche* cakes topped with orange flower-water custard, and some freshly baked *biscuits de Savoie*, featherlight and covered with sliced almonds.

Fresh butter, walnuts, a box of *dragées*—the sugar-coated Savoyard almonds—honey and a selection of *confitures* completed his purchases.

He wondered whether he had forgotten anything. It would be a pity if it were a case of *une économie de bouts de chandelle;* what the English called spoiling the ship for a *sou*'s worth of *goudron*.

Picnics always sounded a good idea, but looking at the carrier-bags he had to admit that not for the first time his eyes had proved bigger than his stomach; a state of affairs that could well be remedied in the not too distant future. On the other hand, Fräulein Brünnhilde looked as though she might prove to be a good trencherwoman. Such a generous figure must need a great deal of sustenance.

He wondered what the incumbents of the Créno-thérapie on the hill behind him would think if they could see his shopping list. Would it make them turn restlessly on their couches behind the glass windows of the sun terraces as they lay back paying the penalty of overstraining their kidneys?

A few sparrows possessed of a courage handed down over the years and honed by constant sorties on the tabletops of the *café*, hopped on to the top of the carrier-bag and clung within pecking distance of the *baguette*, eyeing it hungrily. They scattered as Pommes Frites lifted his head and gave them a warning stare, only to regroup and return to the attack a moment later. Refusing to be baited for the sake of a crumb, Pommes Frites treated them with the contempt they deserved.

Fräulein Brünnhilde was something of an enigma. That she and the person he'd encountered in the wood on the first night were one and the same, he didn't doubt for a moment. Unless the local waters were good for more than kidney trouble and arthritis, there couldn't be another like her in the area; it would be a grossly unfair distribution of national wealth. But if they were one and the same, why had she been lurking there? And why had she turned tail and run? She didn't look the sort of person who would retreat in the face of danger; rather the reverse. The person he'd met at the school would have been much more likely to have hit him over the head with her *sac*. And how had she got there? By her own admission she didn't own a car.

A boat from Lausanne—the *Général Guisan*—gave a warning blast on its foghorn as it swept through the narrow entrance to the harbour, leaving swans and ducks bobbing aggrievedly in its wake. Docking it immaculately, as he must have done thousands of times before, the captain looked out from his bridge across the rooftop of the booking hall, making sure everything was in its place. There was a loud clang as the gangplank dropped into place and a flurry of movement from the waiting passengers as they queued ready to board. A woman carrying a bag of shopping broke into a trot as the traffic lights changed and she hurried across the road to catch the boat. Seeing her from the bridge, the captain blew his foghorn again, anxious to be on his way.

Monsieur Pamplemousse wondered if he was doing the right thing. It could be a total waste of time; a dead end. He was simply playing a hunch that he would be hard put to justify if it came to the point. He could picture the kind of conversation he might have if the Director got to hear about it, especially if he ever caught a glimpse of Fräulein Brünnhilde. His own experience of the printing trade was fairly limited, but he had to admit that she was not the kind of vision he would have conjured up had he been called on to describe a typical representative.

Monsieur Pamplemousse felt in an inside jacket pocket and took out an envelope containing the pasted-up version of the words he'd put together two nights before. The message was clear enough: INFORM POLICE MY LIFE IS IN DANGRE. DO NOT HURRY, AWAAIT NEXT MESSEGE OF YOUR LOVED ONE.

It was a strange message; there was an inconsistency about it which he found bothering. If Jean-Claude had had a premonition that his own life might be in danger, why hadn't he told someone, or simply written the message out himself? Why go to the trouble of making it anonymous by having fake pieces of newsprint made up? They had to be fake; no one could possibly have published them as they were. Then again, why ask for the police to be informed and in the next sentence say 'Do not hurry'? It didn't make sense. And if Jean-Claude hadn't been alarmed on his own account, who could the message have been meant for? The girl? He'd seen her twice now with his own eyes, alive and well and unharmed. She looked worried, that was true, but if she and Jean-

Claude were involved in some way then it was likely to be on his account rather than her own. And how did Fräulein Brünnhilde fit into it all?

There was a movement from under the table and Pommes Frites' head appeared. Monsieur Pamplemousse reached down and patted it. The top felt warm from the sun. Normally Pommes Frites would have been content to sit where he was for a while, basking in his master's attention. Pommes Frites liked nothing better than a good stroke. Given the chance he could put up with being stroked for hours at a time, but for reasons best known to himself he shook his head free and as he stood up, applied the end of his nose to the piece of paper on top of the table. He rested it there for a while, the tip quivering as it absorbed such items of olfactory information as there were to be gained; forwarding them on to the appropriate department for analysis and comparison checks before making a final decision; weighing the results against the obvious needs of his master—the depth of the furrows in his brow, the look of preoccupation which always appeared when he had a problem.

The information duly processed to his satisfaction, the print-out deposited in the tray marked ACTION, Pommes Frites turned and made his way slowly but purposefully in the direction of the exit. Pocketing the sheet of paper, Monsieur Pamplemousse picked up his carrier-bags and followed on behind. He knew better than to query his companion and aide-de-camp at such moments. If Pommes Frites had decided there were trails to be followed, then followed they must be.

In the event, he hadn't far to go; it was hardly worth picking up his belongings. Pommes Frites led the way down a short flight of steps on to the pavement below, wisely hurried past some more steps leading down further to a *W.C. public,* then stopped outside a *tabac-journaux* on the corner. Outside there was a rack of *journaux* neatly arranged according to nationality. Ignoring the ubiquitous *Herald-Tribune,* bypassing Allemagne and Italie, he settled on a section devoted to those from Grande-Bretagne. Rejecting both *The Times* and its pink counterpart devoted to financial matters, registering disapproval of both the *Express* and the *Daily Mail,* declining a fifth, testing a sixth and finding it wanting, he placed his paw very firmly on the one of his choice and gazed up at his master.

Monsieur Pamplemousse patted his head, removed the *journal* from the rack, paid for it in the shop, then made his way back upstairs again and called for another *café.*

He felt a growing excitement as he compared the typeface and the quality of the paper of his purchase with the original. It matched exactly. Running through the rest of the pages quickly it seemed to have the same kind of errors; sometimes it was simply a matter of words omitted or transposed, sometimes whole lines were missing. Once or twice there was an area of complete gibberish. Excitement gave way to confusion.

Paying for his *café* when it arrived, he settled down and considered the matter through half-closed eyes. If the message he had in his hand had been taken from a genuine *journal,* then it put paid to his original theory that the words had been specially printed, which in a sense put him right back where he'd started from. On the other hand, if someone had gone to the trouble of buying an English newspaper, then the message was clearly meant to be read by English eyes. Elementary, my dear Watson, as Holmes would have said.

His own Watson, having done his bit for the time being, had curled up and gone back to sleep in a nearby patch of sunshine.

On the far side of the road, near the traffic lights, there was a squeal of protesting rubber followed by a loud blare from a car horn. A motorist was complaining at being cut-up by a taxi which had pulled in sharply behind another at a rank outside the port building. There was an exchange of gestures, then the lights changed and the aggrieved motorist was forced to give up the contest. The taxi driver, wholly indifferent, climbed out of his cab and joined his colleague on the pavement.

Monsieur Pamplemousse sat up, cursing his stupidity. In pondering the problem of transportation to and from the Institut des Beaux Arbres he'd considered every possibility from *bicyclettes* to lifts thumbed in *voitures* and back again via *tracteurs* and bulldozers. The one method which hadn't crossed his mind was that of hiring a taxi. He drained his cup. He must be getting old.

This time it was his turn to lead the way down the steps. He took them two at a time.

'Do I make many journeys to the Institut des Beaux Arbres?' The first driver looked him straight in the eye. 'I am afraid I do not understand the question, *Monsieur.*'

Monsieur Pamplemousse felt in his wallet, separating a fifty-franc note from some adjacent hundreds.

'What is it you wish to know, *Monsieur*?'

'Do many people make use of your services? Visitors? Staff? Anything you can tell me?'

The man shrugged. 'Most of the staff have their own cars. So do the visitors. Occasionally we get a call from the *gare* if someone arrives by train.'

'How about the girls?'

The two men exchanged glances. 'May we ask why you want to know?' asked the second driver. 'We do not wish to get anyone into trouble.'

Nor would you wish to lose a lucrative business by the sound of it, thought Monsieur Pamplemousse. He decided to press his luck a bit further, hoping they wouldn't ask him for his identification.

'I suggest it will be better in the long run if you tell me the truth.'

The first driver broke the silence. 'Mostly it is girls playing truant. They want to be taken to the disco at Thonon. Sometimes even as far as Geneva. There is a rendezvous point not far from the school. They are young and anxious to enjoy life, you understand? Almost always they go in groups.'

'I understand.' Monsieur Pamplemousse opened his wallet again. Disappointment registered on both faces as he took out the photograph.

'Do you recognise this face? Did she travel with friends or was she alone?'

The two men scanned the photograph uneasily. 'I want to help her. It is possible she may be in trouble.'

'She made the journey often,' said the second man. 'She used to meet a friend here in Evian. They perhaps went for a walk along the front or had a *café* over the road where you had yours.'

'Was the friend Jean-Claude from Les Cinq Parfaits?'

The question went home and gave him match point. Jean-Claude and the girl had been meeting nearly every day, just for short periods in the afternoon when Jean-Claude could leave his work, after *déjeuner* had been served and before it was time to prepare the evening meal. Occasionally she went to the restaurant to eat, but mostly they met in the afternoons. Everyone knew. It was a very happy affair. Jean-Claude always brought her flowers. No, they had never taken Jean-Claude to the school. Anyway, he had his own car, so what would be the point? There were, of course, other drivers, and who knew? It was accompanied by a shrug as if to imply that some people would do anything for money. The information came pouring out. He almost asked for his fifty francs back.

*Monsieur* would not be taking the matter further? Not that they had ever done any harm. But a fare was a fare and out of season business was slow. They could do with all the work they could get.

Monsieur Pamplemousse drove slowly and carefully back to Les Cinq Parfaits, partly because he was deep in thought, partly because the repair to his braking-system was only temporary and he still had to rely a great deal on the handbrake.

He took a turn off the main driveway and parked near his room. Feeling in need of a stroll in order to collect his scattered thoughts and marshal them into some kind of order, he set off with Pommes Frites along the same path he had taken the first evening. As they drew near the edge of the woods a *gendarme* detached himself from a tree, obviously intending to intercept them. Calling to Pommes Frites, Monsieur

Pamplemousse hurriedly retraced his steps. For the time being he didn't want to talk to anyone, least of all the police. They would only ask questions and before that happened he had one or two questions of his own to ask, questions that called for a succession of telephone calls.

Relieved that he hadn't bothered to return his key to Reception that morning, he slipped in through the side entrance.

His first call was to a Mr. Pickering of Burgess Hill in England, and after two wrong numbers, including a housewife who accused him, not without a trace of hope in her voice, of making obscene telephone calls, he eventually got through.

For some while *Le Guide* had been toying with the idea of following the lead set many years before by their arch rival Michelin, and issuing a guide to restaurants in the British Isles. The failure of Gault Millau, who had also tried out the idea and had then withdrawn to lick their wounds on safer ground, gave them second thoughts. It appeared on preliminary investigation that British restaurants had enormous subdivisions, reflecting both the diverse nature of the population and its eating habits. Unlike France, where the local restaurant was often an extension of the home, a place where the whole family from *grand-mère* to the smallest *enfant* could go for Sunday lunch, and where everything from weddings to christenings was celebrated, eating out was more of a treat, a special occasion, and the menu was constructed accordingly. Classification was difficult.

In all these matters, Mr. Pickering, who had been retained as an adviser on account of his vast and expert knowledge of wine, was a fountain of information, as indeed he was on many other things. Had the guillotine been reintroduced in France, Mr. Pickering would have known the exact weight of blade necessary, the degree of sharpness required, and the height from which it needed to be dropped for a given thickness of neck. Had the Roman penchant for eating dormice been revived in England, Mr. Pickering would have known all about ways of fattening them first on nuts in earthenware jars, how they should be stuffed, and the correct method of cooking them. 'Regulo 5 for fifteen minutes' he would probably have said in tones of unimpeachable authority.

Monsieur Pamplemousse had learned a lot about the British since he'd met Mr. Pickering. He felt sure he would know all there was to know about English *journaux*. In this he was not disappointed. From a brief description of the nature and the type of the cuttings, and with scarcely a moment's hesitation, Mr. Pickering named it at once.

'They have a bad record of industrial disputes. Progress is not easy in the printing world. There is a great deal of unrest within the rank and file regarding the introduction of new machinery. Meanwhile the owners soldier on with the old equipment.'

'You mean . . . it is actually sold like that? The one I have is not just an early edition—an uncorrected one? They are all like it?' Monsieur Pamplemousse tried to keep a rising note of disappointment from his voice.

'It has a circulation of several million. People get very upset on days when it doesn't appear.'

'Several million? *Morbleu!* Do the readers not care for their language?'

'Frankly, no.' Mr. Pickering sounded surprised by the question. 'In a way it makes the news more palatable if you don't entirely understand it. It leaves you with hope for the future. Life would be unbearable if you knew all that was going on.'

'They do not mind the mistakes . . . the misprints?'

'They rather like them really. It makes it more fun to read. Besides, it's been that way for a long time and the British don't really like change. Sometimes they write to the editor about it, but on the whole the mistakes are in the political area—parliamentary reports—things like that. You don't often find them on the sports pages—there would be hell to pay if you did, and *never* in the crossword.'

Monsieur Pamplemousse felt bemused and quite out of his depth. No wonder Britain wasn't popular with the other members of the Common Market if that was all they cared about politics.

'And if I were looking for a lady compositor?'

Mr. Pickering gave vent to a series of clicks. It sounded as though he was tapping his teeth with a pen. 'Very unlikely. The printing industry is a closed shop—very much a man's world. I can't picture them allowing women in.

'Talking of crosswords, it's funny you should ring. I was only thinking about you a moment ago. I've got a sort of French clue in front of me right now . . . "A bad-tempered worker gains in the beginning and gets something to eat". Nine letters.'

Monsieur Pamplemousse fell silent. He had enough problems on his mind as it was without adding to them with trivialities.

'I'll put you out of your misery,' said Mr. Pickering cheerfully. 'It's a sort of anagram. Cross means bad-tempered. An ant is a worker. "I" is the first letter of "in". Put the "i" into "cross" and add the "ant" and you get *croissant*—something to eat.'

'I, too, have a sort of anagram,' said Monsieur Pamplemousse, not wishing to be outdone. He removed the pasted-up message from his wallet and read out the words, jumbling them up in no particular order as he did so.

'Don't tell me,' said Mr. Pickering. 'I like puzzles. I'll ring you back when I've got it.'

'I shall be going out again in about half an hour,' said Monsieur Pamplemousse, throwing down the gauntlet.

'Done!' said Mr. Pickering.

The second call was to an ex-colleague in Paris.

'The Institut des Beaux Arbres? What is it you wish to know exactly?'

'Anything,' said Monsieur Pamplemousse. 'If there is nothing, then I wish to know that too. Anything and everything or nothing.'

His third call was to the Director. Almost immediately he wished he hadn't made it, but it was too late to hang up. The voice at the other end sounded ominously brisk.

'Good, Pamplemousse. You have my telex.'

'No, *Monsieur*.'

'You do not have my telex?' The Director sounded piqued. 'But I sent it to you first thing this morning. It *must* have been received. That is the whole point of using a telex machine—the knowledge that a message accepted has, ergo, been received.'

'It may have been received by Reception,' said Monsieur Pamplemousse patiently, 'but I have not, myself, been to Reception. I have been out shopping.'

'You have been out shopping?' The Director repeated the words in the same tones of awe tempered with disbelief that Mrs. Newton might have used when her husband Isaac came in from the garden and announced that he had just discovered gravity.

'I have been making progress, *Monsieur*. The shopping was a necessary part of a plan I am about to put into operation, a plan which . . .'

'Pamplemousse.' The Director's voice cut him off peevishly in midflight. 'Had you been to Reception this morning, and had you picked up the telex message I was at great pains to send, you would have saved yourself a journey and *Le Guide,* I suspect from the tone of your voice, a great deal of expense; expense which in the circumstances I may find hard to justify when it comes to initialling your P39s.'

Pique changed to irony. 'To save you the trouble of going all the way to Reception, I will read you my message. It said, quite simply: CANCEL ORDER FOR *SOUFFLÉ SURPRISE* IMMEDIATELY.'

'Cancel the order for the *Soufflé Surprise*? I do not understand, *Monsieur*.' He understood full well, but he wasn't going to make things easy for the Director.

'It is perfectly simple, Pamplemousse. There is no longer any cause for alarm. Progress has been made. Some of the best chefs in France have been working on the problem. I cannot go into details, of course, but if I were to mention names like Bocuse, Vergé, Guérard, you will understand the importance attached to the matter. The end result is not quite like the real thing—that would be very difficult in the time, but I think I may safely say that it is good enough.' Monsieur Pamplemousse thought he detected a sound of smacking lips in the background, and murmurs of agreement. It was rubbing salt into the wound.

'But what about Jean-Claude?'

'Jean-Claude?' The Director brushed the name aside airily as if it were of no importance. 'I'm sure he will turn up eventually.'

Monsieur Pamplemousse took the photograph from his wallet once again and propped it against the telephone for moral support. Was it his imagination or did the face looking back at him have a pleading look? Perhaps it was simply that he now had another picture in his mind, an image of the real thing he was able to superimpose on the first, breathing life into it. He came to a decision.

'That is not good enough, *Monsieur*.'

'What? What is that, Pamplemousse?' The Director broke off from a dissertation he'd been about to give on the problems involved in injecting the right amount of *surprise* into a *soufflé*.

'I said, *Monsieur*, that it is not good enough. There are things going on here which I do not understand.'

'There are things going on everywhere that *I* do not understand, Pamplemousse.' The Director came back down to earth again. 'I have to say, quite frankly, that there are things I do not even *wish* to understand. Things I would rather not know about. But that does not mean to say that I feel it my duty to put them to rights. The world is an imperfect place, Aristide. It has always been so and despite everyone's efforts, so it will remain. That is not necessarily a bad thing. Perfection, taken to excess, can be very dull and boring.'

'Do I take it, *Monsieur*, that I no longer have your support in this matter?'

'If you wish to put it that way, Aristide, yes. I have my orders too. Orders, Pamplemousse, which emanate from an authority even higher than the earlier one. To put it crudely I have been told to tell you to lay off. You have been seen visiting the Institut des Beaux Arbres. That was not part of your original brief. Your brief was to find Jean-Claude.'

'It is my opinion, *Monsieur*, that the two are linked.'

'Pamplemousse . . . you have your orders.'

'I am afraid I do not accept them, *Monsieur*.'

There was a violent explosion from the other end. It sounded as though a desk was being thumped. When the noise died away the Director's voice came through loud and clear and in measured tones.

'Pamplemousse, I have to tell you that if you persist in this stubborn attitude, then you will be on your own. You will get no help from anyone. You will be *persona non grata*. Worse still, you may well find your name besmirched in ways which will make your escapade at the Follies seem like a visit to Papa Noël.'

'So be it, *Monsieur*.' Monsieur Pamplemousse hung up before the Director had a chance to say any more. He was about to take the receiver off the hook again when he remembered he was expecting a different call to be returned and changed his mind.

He hadn't long to wait.

The telephone rang three times in quick succession. The first call was from Paris.

'Guillard here. This Institut you asked me about . . . you might have said.'

'Said what?'

'Well, it's pretty hot stuff. No one wants to talk about it and I've already had all sorts of people phoning me back wanting to know why I was asking in the first place.'

'Did you tell them?'

'No. I thought you'd rather I didn't so I concocted a cock and bull story about wanting to know for a friend. I think they bought it.'

'*D'accord*.' Monsieur Pamplemousse knew the feeling.

'Anyway, I eventually got on to someone I know at the Ministry and it seems they have an appalling accident record. *Incroyable*. It is hard to believe. Nine girls over the past two years. The worst was in an avalanche last winter. The instructors managed to get away, but three of the girls were killed. Two went missing soon afterwards in Lac Léman—presumed drowned. Two more disappeared the year before during an outing to Rome. One ran away and was never seen again. Another one fell down a disused mine shaft.'

'And nothing's been heard of any of them since? No bodies have been found?'

'Nothing at all. They all vanished without trace.'

'Thank you.'

'That's all right. Sorry I couldn't be of any more help.'

'You have done very well. I am most grateful.' He was about to hang up when a thought struck him. 'You don't happen to know the colour of their hair? The ones who disappeared, that is.'

'*Sapristi!*' There was a muttered oath from the other end. 'You will be wanting to know the colour of their nail-varnish next. I'm in enough trouble as it is.'

'*Tant pis*. Never mind.'

He hung up. It had been worth a try. A shot in the dark.

The second call was from England.

'I say . . . you've been busy. I've tried about six times. The line's always engaged.' Mr. Pickering sounded pleased with himself.

'You have thought of something else?'

'No. It's just that I have the answer to that word puzzle you gave me. Didn't take a couple of minutes actually. How's this? HURRY—LIFE OF YOUR LOVED ONE IS IN DANGER. DO NOT INFORM POLICE. AWAIT MY NEXT MESSAGE.

'Hello . . . I say, are you still there?'

'Yes, I am still here.' Monsieur Pamplemousse reached mechanically for his pen. 'Would you mind repeating that?'

Pickering obliged. 'Forgive my asking . . . none of my business . . . but it all sounds very intriguing.'

Monsieur Pamplemousse refused to be drawn. 'It is a little *divertissement*. I will tell you about it one day.'

Mr. Pickering took the hint. 'Au revoir, Aristide. Take care.'

'*Au revoir*, Monsieur Pickering. And congratulations.'

Leaving Mr. Pickering to his crossword puzzle, Monsieur Pamplemousse replaced the receiver and crossed to the window. He slid it open. Outside on the terrace the waiters were preparing the tables for lunch. Beyond them, near the entrance, there was a parked police car. It was empty. Near the path leading to the wood the *gendarme* had been replaced by two members of the National Guard, automatic weapons slung over their shoulders at the ready.

Mr. Pickering's rearrangement of the words put a totally different complexion on things. It very definitely turned the message into one which was designed for someone else to send or to be sent on someone else's behalf. Someone already missing, or someone about to go missing?

Turning away from the window he idly picked up his camera from the desk where he'd left it the night before and cocked it ready for the next shot. He had a feeling he might be needing it. The rewind crank didn't move. Either there was slack in the film, which was strange in view of the fact that he was already halfway through a reel, or . . . he cocked the shutter again, then a third time. Still there was no movement. He flipped the back open. The camera chamber was empty.

In the waste-bin below the table he found a roll of film. It had been completely pulled out of the cassette. The Department of Dirty Tricks had been at it again.

The telephone rang for the third time. Blissfully unaware that he had chosen an unfortunate moment, the Director launched into an apology.

'Aristide, I'm glad I caught you. I'm sorry if I lost my temper a moment ago.'

'We all lose our temper from time to time, *Monsieur*. I am about to lose mine.'

'I'm afraid I was not feeling myself, Aristide. A touch of the *furibards*. Too much *soufflé*, you understand? We have been up all night, tasting, tasting, tasting. Also, I was not alone.'

'I understand perfectly, *Monsieur*. While you have been sitting in your office eating *Soufflé Surprise*, others have been busy entering my room—removing film from my camera. While you were enjoying your gastronomic excursions, others were busy sawing through the main pipeline of the hydraulic brakes of my car.'

'What is that?' The Director grasped the nettle with both hands. 'This is terrible, Aristide. Had something happened to you—and to Pommes Frites—I would never have forgiven myself. Thank heaven you discovered it in time.'

'We did *not* discover it in time, *Monsieur*. Pommes Frites and I are lucky to be alive. Had it not been for a road sign which got in the way . . .'

'A road sign? You collided with a road sign? Is there much damage?'

'A new bumper, perhaps. Possibly a new wing. Fortunately with the 2CV it is only a matter of replacement. That is one of its many virtues.'

The Director made a clicking noise. 'This is bad news, Aristide. Very bad news indeed. As you well know, it is the policy of *Le Guide* to require all staff to make use of the standard issue of *voiture*. It is why I visit the Paris Motor Show every year. A special dispensation was granted in your case provided no unnecessary and untoward expense was incurred. Madame Grante will not be pleased. It may be necessary to review the whole situation in the light of what you have just told me.'

Monsieur Pamplemousse took a deep breath. '*Baiser* Madame Grante!'

There was a moment's silence while the Director digested the remark. 'An interesting thought, Aristide.' His voice sounded milder, almost affectionate. 'Not one that appeals to me, I must admit. Sooner you than me. Apart from anything else, who knows what hidden passions you might release. Passions kept in check over the years by constant scanning of P39s.'

'One moment, *Monsieur*.' From outside, beyond the trees, came the sound of a helicopter approaching fast. Fast and low. The noise made it difficult to hear what the Director was saying.

Monsieur Pamplemousse crossed to the window, cupping the telephone receiver under his chin as he did so. The two National Guardsmen were in a state of alert, their machine-guns at the ready as they watched the sky in an area beyond the pool where the tops of the trees were already waving in the down-draught from the plane. The waiters had all stopped work and were watching too. The two coloured boys from Reception hurried past pulling a trolley on which reposed a large roll of carpet. Monsieur Pamplemousse slid the window shut. The director was still talking.

'I cannot persuade you to change your mind?'

'No; *Monsieur*.'

'I sometimes wish I had your sense of right and wrong, Pamplemousse. It is an enviable trait.'

'*Comme ci, comme ça, Monsieur.* Sometimes it is a blessing, at other times it is a curse.'

'Pamplemousse . . .'

'*Oui, Monsieur?*'

'I do not know what you have in mind, and perhaps it is better that I do not ask. Also, I should not be telling you this—it is supposed to be secret—but the "shopping expedition" of a "certain person" has been brought forward for security reasons. He is due to arrive at Les Cinq Parfaits today.'

'I think, *Monsieur*, he is arriving at this very moment.'

'*Alors!*' The Director sounded depressed. 'In that case, Aristide, I can only wish you *bonne chance*.'

'*Merci, Monsieur.*'

As he hung up, Monsieur Pamplemousse glanced at his watch. It was just after twelve thirty. If he was to be on time for his meeting with Fräulein Brünnhilde he would need to leave at once.

He crossed to the fridge and opened the door. The room maid had obviously completed her rounds, for the rack of apéritifs and mineral waters had been restocked, but the bottle of champagne he'd ordered was nowhere to be seen. Worse still, the second bottle of Château d'Yquem seemed to have vanished.

'*Merde!*' He was about to close the door again in disgust when he paused and looked in the freezer compartment. A bottle bearing the Gosset label lay on top of the icetray awaiting his pleasure, but there was still no sign of the d'Yquem. It must have been put somewhere for safekeeping—such riches demanded special treatment. Lifting the champagne carefully out of the compartment he examined the bottle. He could hardly grumble, since he'd asked for it to be as cold as possible, but it was now so cold that the outside was white with ice. He glanced at the freezer control—it had been turned to maximum. He would need to treat the champagne with respect; in its present state it could be lethal.

Closing the door of the fridge, he took the cardboard tube out of its carrier-bag and slid the bottle gently inside it. It fitted as snugly as if it had been made to measure.

Seeing his master reach for the other carrier-bag, Pommes Frites leapt to his feet. Pommes Frites liked picnics and one way and another he had a lot of eating to catch up on. That apart, Monsieur Pamplemousse's mood communicated itself to him in no uncertain manner. Second only to food, Pommes Frites enjoyed nothing better than a spot of action. He licked his lips. All his senses told him that with a little bit of luck he could be enjoying both before he was very much older.

# 7

## THE PICNIC

THE JOURNEY TO LES BEAUX ARBRES TOOK MONsieur Pamplemousse even longer than it had on the first occasion, mostly because of the state of his car. With its 150,000-kilometre service long overdue and the pads on the cable-operated front-wheel brakes now even more badly in need of replacement following the sabotage of the main system, he had no wish to stop on a steep part of the hill. If they once started rolling backwards there was no knowing where they would end up. He could hardly hope for another convenient road sign to get in their way, and the bottom of the valley looked too far away for comfort.

Fräulein Brünnhilde was waiting for them behind some bushes. She was dressed in a brightly coloured, transparently thin cotton skirt, topped rather disappointingly by a tee-shirt bearing a map of North America. Her blonde hair was tightly coiffeured into a neat but forbidding bun. Paradoxically, she was carrying what appeared to be a groundsheet under her arm.

'It is for the picnic,' she announced as she climbed into the passenger seat.

Monsieur Pamplemousse eyed it uneasily as he helped her on with the seat-belt, adjusting it from N.P.F. (*Normale Pommes Frites*) to a more suitable size—somewhere at the higher end of the scale.

Apart from any untoward implications which might or might not go with the sharing of a groundsheet, he would have much preferred making use of the folding table and chairs which he kept permanently in the boot. In his experience even the lushest of pastureland grew inordinately hard in a matter of moments. That apart, the more inviting it looked the higher the animal population; he'd once seen some incredible figure quoted for just one square metre of earth.

Pommes Frites had even stronger views on the subject of picnics and he gazed disapprovingly at the offending object as it landed on the seat beside him. It was bad enough being relegated to the back of the car without having half of it taken up by what he considered to be highly unnecessary luggage, and he registered his disapproval in no uncertain fashion by breathing heavily down the back of his master's neck. In a matter of moments there was a satisfactory wet patch on the shirt collar.

They had only gone a little way when Fräulein Brünnhilde gave a sudden wriggle. 'I will take shelter while we pass the school gates,' she announced, disappearing below the level of the dashboard with a total disregard as to whether or not her skirt would follow suit. Monsieur Pamplemousse felt a dryness in his throat as he glanced down. Patently it had decided against the idea of accompanying its owner.

Viewed from close quarters, Fräulein Brünnhilde seemed to have grown in stature; the word Amazonian would not be amiss in describing her. The material of her tee-shirt was strained far beyond the limits which might reasonably have been specified by even the most generous of garment manufacturers. From his vantage point in the back seat Pommes Frites followed the direction of his master's gaze and he, too, eyed their passenger with interest. Interest which was tinged, despite his feelings about the groundsheet, with a certain amount of awe.

Thanking his lucky stars that he'd thought to open the roof of the car before they left—it would have been unbearably warm otherwise—Monsieur Pamplemousse glanced up the driveway as they passed the entrance to the school. There was nothing to be seen. The gates were shut.

'You are safe now.'

Fräulein Brünnhilde wriggled herself back up into a sitting position and readjusted the belt, removing a few loose dog hairs as she did so. 'I see you read the English *journaux*,' she said, catching sight of the newspaper lying on the shelf above the dashboard.

Monsieur Pamplemousse felt a quickening of interest as he considered the remark, weighed it, analysed it, and began to wonder if perhaps his original theory had been right after all.

'You are interested in printing?'

'No. What is interesting about printing?' He received an odd look in reply.

'I only wondered, that is all.'

'It is a very strange question. Why do you ask if I am interested in printing?'

Monsieur Pamplemousse began to wish he hadn't. Fräulein Brünnhilde clearly had a very literal turn of mind, the workings of which were not enhanced by her phrase-book style of conversation. He decided he must be patient. In fairness, his own knowledge of German was minimal.

'Your spelling is not good, perhaps?' he asked hopefully.

'My spelling is very good. Why do you say my spelling is not good?'

'Because you would not improve it by reading that particular *journal*,' said Monsieur Pamplemousse with authority.

'Why do you say that? What is wrong with it! It is a very good *journal*.'

'There are many mistakes. Some letters are not where they should be. Sometimes there are whole lines that are not where they should be.' It was catching. Any moment now he would find himself drawing on an old English/French phrase-book he kept handy in case of an emergency. 'You have taken the wrong tooth out!' was one of his favourites. It was almost worth a visit to the dentist to try it out and see what happened.

'I wish to improve my vocabulary. All the girls speak English. It is hard to talk to them. They say things I do not understand, so all the time I am doing the crossword.'

'Ah, the crossword!' Busy with his thoughts, Monsieur Pamplemousse felt the warmth of a body against him as he negotiated a bend too fast. 'A bad-tempered worker gains in the beginning and gets something to eat. Nine letters.'

Fräulein Brünnhilde righted herself. 'What are you saying? I do not understand.'

'It is a clue from an English crossword,' he explained.

'Ah!' Fräulein Brünnhilde nodded. 'And what is the answer?'

'*Croissant.*'

'*Croissant*? I do not understand.'

Monsieur Pamplemousse changed down as they approached an even sharper bend. Ahead of them the Cornettes de Bises loomed large, marking the border between France and Switzerland. 'It has to do with a bad-tempered ant—a worker—and the cross which has an "i" in it.' He heard his voice trail away. He hadn't totally understood the answer himself and it sounded even less probable now.

'Why does the cross have an eye in it?' demanded Fräulein Brünnhilde. 'And why is the ant in a bad mood?'

Monsieur Pamplemousse felt tempted to suggest that perhaps it had been trying to explain crosswords to an idiot foreign ant, but he refrained.

'On Saturdays,' said Fräulein Brünnhilde unexpectedly, 'they have a prize draw. There is a token for the first one they open. With the token you can buy a book. They have never opened one of mine. I have never won a prize.'

'You like reading?'

'No. I do not like reading.'

'In that case,' said Monsieur Pamplemousse, 'it is good that you have never won.' Having delivered this remark he fell silent. The prospect of a picnic with Fräulein Brünnhilde was rapidly losing its attraction.

He glanced across at her. She seemed to be breathing heavily, wriggling uncomfortably from side to side as though she was having complications beneath her tee-shirt. As she leaned forward to carry out some unspecified rearrangements and adjustments behind her back he couldn't help but notice the coastal mountains of California and the Appalachian Mountains of Eastern America resting impressively against the dashboard. Although they were jiggling up and down in time with the motion of the car they had none of the gay abandon one might have expected. Clearly they were being held in place by a superior form of restraint.

Averting his gaze and fixing it firmly on the road ahead, he reached out with his free hand for the safety-belt. 'May I help?'

His offer was rejected in no uncertain fashion.

'Please do not do that!' Fräulein Brünnhilde looked at him severely. 'I have met your sort before.'

Monsieur Pamplemousse wondered where. He felt aggrieved, both by the refusal of what had been intended as a genuine offer of help and by the sweeping generalisation that went with it.

'You are not to touch my top storey. It is *verboten*. You may touch my knees. You may touch my ankles. You may touch my bottom storey. Anything else. But not my top storey.'

Undecided as to whether he had received an invitation, a reproof, or the laying down of a set of architectural guidelines for future reference, Monsieur Pamplemousse lapsed again into silence.

Fräulein Brünnhilde spoke first. 'Are we going much higher?' she enquired. 'Heights give me problems. So do depths. I am best at sea-level.'

Monsieur Pamplemousse found the remark too cryptic even to think about. Holmes might have pondered over it, or perhaps Mr. Pickering. It sounded like one of his crossword clues.

'We are nearly there. I am taking you to a little place I know.'

'Is it where you take all your girls?'

'I have never taken a girl there before in the whole of my life.'

Monsieur Pamplemousse was able to speak with conviction. The only other time he'd been there was with Madame Pamplemousse when they had been exploring the area a few years before, and that was hardly in the same category. He still remembered it; most of all he remembered the profusion of wild flowers. Lower down the valley and on the hillsides fruit was still on the trees waiting to be picked, the grapes were yet to be harvested, but here, high up in the mountains, there would be wild geraniums, harebells, daisies and late crocus amongst the clover.

He turned in past a notice which estimated in hours the time it would take a walker to reach the next vantage point. Breaking off from the narrow track, he drove down a short dip and then up a grassy slope until he reached the top of a ridge where, if his memory served him aright, he knew there would be a view through a gap in the hills to Lac Leman, and beyond that again to mountain-tops eternally covered in ice and snow. He wasn't disappointed. The weather was on his side and the view was breathtaking.

Swinging the car round in a broad circle, he brought it to rest on top of the ridge facing the way they had come, its bonnet pointing back down the hill. Noting a strong smell of burning from the overworked brakelinings, he left it in gear and climbed out, followed by Pommes Frites.

'It is very beautiful here. It is a good choice.' Fräulein Brünnhilde appeared at his side carrying the groundsheet. She breathed in deeply, winced visibly, then touched his elbow with her hand. 'It is very romantic. The lake and the mountains.'

'It has always attracted poets and writers,' said Monsieur Pamplemousse. 'Especially the English ones. English poets are fond of lakes.' He drew on memories of past conversations with Mr. Pickering. 'It was outside the Hotel d'Angleterre at Sécheron that Byron first met Shelley. Another writer, Gibbon, finished a book called *Decline and Fall* at Lausanne.' He pointed towards the gap in the hills. 'Near there, where the lake is at its deepest, Shelley and Byron almost died in a sudden storm.'

Taking the groundsheet he shook it open and began laying it out behind the car. Along its sides there was a series of brass eyelets to which lengths of cord had been attached. He took the ones nearest to the rear bumper and began tying them securely in place, lifting up the edge of the sheet as he did so in order to make a barrier against the light south-westerly breeze.

'It is hard to think of storms on such a day as this. Storms are for bad days.' Fräulein Brünnhilde removed some pins from behind her ears, shaking her head as she did so. Her long, blonde hair glinted in the sunshine as it cascaded down her back. The effect was startling, like the sudden release of a waterfall, the transformation scene in a play.

Monsieur Pamplemousse cleared his throat, aware that Pommes Frites was watching too. He busied himself with a knot. 'Perhaps it was the fault of Shelley himself. Water always had a fascination for him. In the end he died in a boat which had been christened *Don Juan* by Byron.'

Fräulein Brünnhilde looked at him curiously. 'You know a lot about some things.'

'No.' Monsieur Pamplemousse went round to the side of the car and removed the carrier-bags. 'I know a *little* about many things. That is not the same. It has always been one of my problems. I am a picker-up of unconsidered trifles.'

Before closing the door he signalled to Pommes Frites to get back in. There were times when Pommes Frites got in the way if he felt so inclined. Or, not to mince words, if he got an attack of the jealousies. He looked as if he might have a bad one coming on. Pommes Frites obeyed the order with a marked lack of enthusiasm. He climbed into the car wearing his 'hard done by' expression.

Avoiding the unwinking gaze through the back window, Monsieur Pamplemousse began unloading the picnic, crouching as low as possible so as to avoid rubbing too much salt into Pommes Frites' wounds. He stood the bottles of Mondeuse and Evian and the cardboard tube containing the champagne in a neat row in front of the bumper, then reached into the second bag. 'Take this *gâteau de foies blonds de volaille, par exemple.* Some people might say that it does not matter how or where it came from; the fact that it is created from a *poulet de Bresse* means nothing to them. But to me, the knowledge that by law for the whole of its life, it will never have had less than ten square metres of land to itself, to run about on and to feed naturally, will also mean that its flesh will be juicy, and that will sharpen my appetite and thus increase my enjoyment.'

He took out two more packages and held them up. 'Knowing that this ham was smoked over pinewood and juniper berries high up in the mountains where the air is crisp, will add romance to the flavour. And when we follow it with this'—he unwrapped the *Reblochon*—'the knowledge that the word *reblocher* means the last and richest dregs of milk from the cow's udder will not make it any more digestible, but it will warm my heart.'

'You are interested in food?' The thought was evidently a new one.

'If I am fortunate enough to live to be ninety,' said Monsieur Pamplemousse, 'and if I am equally lucky and continue to eat three meals a day it will amount to a grand lifetime's total of over one hundred thousand meals. It would be foolish not to be interested in something which has occupied so great a part of one's life and is in part responsible for its continuation. It would be even worse than economising on the bed in which one spends perhaps a third of one's existence.'

Fräulein Brünnhilde lowered herself carefully on to the groundsheet and lay back staring up at the sky. She appeared to be encountering a certain amount of difficulty in carrying out the manoeuvre, rather as if some hidden and opposing forces were at work, but at least she made herself comfortable.

'For me, sunshine is more important. That, to me, is food. Anything is better than being at the Institut.'

'Tell me about the Institut.'

She made a face. 'It is not interesting.'

'Everything is interesting,' said Monsieur Pamplemousse. 'I told you. I am a picker-up of unconsidered trifles. Tell me, for example, about the Sanatorium.'

Fräulein Brünnhilde sat up. 'Ah! You have chosen the worst thing. That is not a trifle. For three whole days I have been forbidden to enter my own sick bay. And for why?'

'For why?' said Monsieur Pamplemousse gently.

'I think it is that they do not trust me. There is something happening there they do not wish me to know about. But I will find out.' As she spoke, Fräulein Brünnhilde tapped her chest. For a brief moment she seemed to regret the action, then she recovered.

'In here I have a key. They do not know that. They have already taken away what they think is the only one. But in here I have a spare.'

Monsieur Pamplemousse eyed her thoughtfully. A key to the sick bay was what he most wanted at that moment. He had a feeling it would unlock many other doors besides. Getting hold of it might be another matter.

Reaching for a bottle of Evian he tore off the seal, removed the plastic top and slowly poured two glassfuls, adding some ice from the container for good measure.

As Fräulein Brünnhilde reached over to take one of the glasses her tee-shirt parted company with her skirt, leaving a large gap. For a brief moment he toyed with the idea of making a quick reconnaissance in the direction of Louisiana, a sudden pincer movement to establish what geographical problems any major invasion might encounter in Arkansas and beyond. But he was immediately forestalled. Fräulein Brünnhilde drew back, raising her glass as she did so.

'*Prost!*'

'*Balcons!*' It was a Freudian slip and one he immediately regretted. Fräulein Brünnhilde drew back still further. The moment had passed.

'You are thinking bad thoughts,' she said reprovingly. 'You are what is called a *tétons* man.'

'I am a man,' said Monsieur Pamplemousse simply, meeting directness with directness.

'Ah, men!' Fräulein Brünnhilde managed to invest in the word a wealth of meaning, not all of it bad. There was a certain wistfulness too.

'I appreciate the beauties of nature when I see them,' said Monsieur Pamplemousse defensively, 'and I like to savour them. If you were to ask a mountaineer "why do you wish to climb Mount Everest?" the answer would be simple. He would say "because it is there". To him that would be sufficient reason.'

'It is not sufficient reason in my case,' said Fräulein Brünnhilde firmly. She watched Monsieur Pamplemousse warily over the top of her glass as he busied himself laying out the rest of the picnic.

'The Herr Professor is a *tétons* man. He pretends he is a nature-lover, but he watches the girls with his binoculars through the changing-room window. He thinks no one knows. But I have seen him. I tell the girls they must keep their leotards on at all times.'

'Perhaps,' said Monsieur Pamplemousse, 'he is frustrated.' He helped himself surreptitiously to a *dragée*. Being surrounded day and night by nubile nineteen year olds must have its problems. Other diversions around the Institut des Beaux Arbres seemed conspicuous by their absence. He was glad he had left his own binoculars back at the hotel. Fräulein Brünnhilde might think the worst.

'*He* is frustrated? What about me? *I* am frustrated. You do not know what it is like being there all day long with no one to talk to except a lot of young girls.'

'Why did you go there?'

'I saw an advertisement in a German newspaper. It seemed a good idea at the time. Now, I do not think so any more. I do not like it there. I am unhappy. I am too much alone. Night-times are the worst.'

'What about the other men?'

'There are no other men.'

'Not even the ski instructors?'

'They are not there in the summer. They only return about now. Besides, they are different. I do not trust them.'

Monsieur Pamplemousse found himself wondering why. Perhaps in the Fräulein's eyes all men were alike, only some were more so. If the girls he'd come across the day before were anything to go by, he could see why the ski instructors had made such a contented group in the photograph. They had it made. And yet, contentment was a word which had many connotations. There had been something else as well. Some element he couldn't quite put his finger on. A certain hardness. As a parent he wouldn't have been entirely happy.

'I will ask you another question.' Fräulein Brünnhilde broke into his thoughts. 'Why is it that all the girls are blonde? Why are there no brunettes? Why are there no redheads?'

Monsieur Pamplemousse fell silent. It was quite true. At first he had only half-registered the fact without actually giving it much thought, but subconsciously it had prompted his query to Guillard.

'Perhaps,' he said without conviction, 'it is a coincidence.'

'Perhaps,' said Fräulein Brünnhilde complacently as she lay back and folded her hands across her stomach. 'Perhaps not.'

Monsieur Pamplemousse leaned over to remove the glass to a position of safety, and as he did so he became aware of a strange phenomenon, a kind of amalgam of movement, of undulating breasts and rising and falling hands which didn't entirely relate to each other. It was hard to rationalise the feeling, but once again he was left with a distinct impression of opposing forces at work. He was also only too well aware of the fact that both tee-shirt and skirt were now very far apart indeed. Flesh, bare, white, warm, patently alive, lay within his grasp. He caught a glimpse of something metal.

It might be worth a try. The thing was if he tried and failed—if the key was attached to a chain, perhaps even some kind of primitive burglar alarm (and he wouldn't put it past her)—he might never get another chance.

Placing the glass down on the groundsheet out of harm's way, he was about to shift his position a little when he glanced up and realised that Pommes Frites was watching his every movement through the rear window of the car. Back paws straining against the dashboard, he was craning precariously across the back of the seats as he sought to obtain a ringside view of all that was going on. As he caught Monsieur Pamplemousse's eye he assumed one of his enigmatic expressions. When he chose, Pommes Frites could look very puritanical. It was something to do with the folds of the skin on his face and the deep-set eyes. Given suitable headgear he might well, at that moment, have passed for a Pilgrim Father catching his first glimpse of Massachusetts U.S.A. through a porthole in the side of the *Mayflower* and not caring overmuch for what he saw. It was, to say the least, very offputting.

All the thoughts of making a frontal assault on Fräulein Brünnhilde were dashed from Monsieur Pamplemousse's mind. He eased himself back to his original position, wondering if perhaps it might be as well to prepare the ground a little.

'Would you care for a glass of champagne?'

'That would be very good.' She stirred lazily, almost disappointedly.

Pommes Frites watched with renewed interest as his master leaned back and reached over his shoulder.

It was, as it happened, the last coherent act any of them were to perform for some little time to come.

The peace of la Dent d'Oche was suddenly shattered by a violent explosion and Monsieur Pamplemousse felt the cardboard tube wrenched from his hand.

A passing *vigneron* from Epernay would have put his finger on the cause of the explosion right away. Given all the facts, a junior science master would have launched into a stern lecture on the inadvisability of storing champagne in the freezer compartment of a refrigerator rather than the rack inside the door. In normal circumstances, and given more time at his disposal, it would be true to say that even Monsieur Pamplemousse would have speedily put two and two together.

Gaseous liquid, solidified after its spell in the *frigo*, slowly warmed by the autumn sun, thoroughly shaken during the long and bumpy drive up the mountain, had come to life again, building up a pressure far in excess of its accepted norm of seven atmospheres, before finally rebelling.

That the bottle hadn't burst en route was a tribute not only to its makers, but also to those who had followed on in the wake of Dom Perignon, perfecting over the years the art of layering and gluing together bark from the Spanish *Quercus suber,* inventing machines capable of squeezing the resultant cork into something like half its size so that it could be driven into the neck of the bottle by a powerhammer, free to expand once again before being held in place by the wire *muselet.*

But there is a limit to everything. Unable to withstand the enormous pressures a moment longer, the bottle had, at Monsieur Pamplemousse's sudden movement, parted company with its base. Left to its own devices, it emerged from the tube in a manner which would have merited a spontaneous round of applause from Cape Canaveral.

Monsieur Pamplemousse's reaction was both swift and dramatic. Convinced that it was yet another attempt on his life by the Department of Dirty Tricks, deprived of any such nicety as a countdown, he automatically made a dive for the figure at his side, throwing his whole body on top in an effort to protect it. As he landed he felt a sharp pain in his chest. There was a gasp followed almost immediately by another, smaller explosion from somewhere beneath him. A low rumbling noise and what felt like the beginnings of an earthquake added to the confusion. Arms and legs encircled his body, holding him in a vice-like grip from which there was no escape, whilst a scream in his left ear momentarily blotted out any attempt at rationalising the situation.

Reaching out in desperation, he grabbed at the nearest available object, and as the rumblings and shakings and bumps grew worse with every passing second, held on to it for dear life.

But if the reasons for the original explosion were complex, the cause of the volcanic-like eruption beneath the groundsheet was easier to pin down. Pommes Frites could have put his paw on the cause immediately. Or, to put it another way, one of his paws had triggered it off.

Not usually given to emotional outbursts, trained like his master not to show fear in the face of danger, Pommes Frites had been so startled by the explosion that in his haste to get clear he had used the gear lever as a springboard, pushing it into neutral as he executed a leap into the air of such Olympic proportions it had caused him to sail clean through the sunshine-roof.

The result was almost as spectacular as the cause and he stood watching the progress of events, looking increasingly unhappy as the car gathered speed and disappeared down the hill taking the groundsheet and its picnickers with it. He winced visibly as the car collided with a tree in the dip at the bottom and came to an abrupt halt.

For a moment he toyed with the idea of going for a walk. It was a nice day and he had an uneasy feeling his master would not be in a very good mood. But only for a moment. Loyalty coupled with a desire to find out what was going on finally won the day and he set off down the hill as fast as he could go.

Pommes Frites arrived on the scene just in time to

see his master let go of the bumper and make an abortive effort to struggle into a sitting position. It was an attempt which was doomed to failure. Fräulein Brünnhilde's arms were still locked firmly in position.

Monsieur Pamplemousse gazed down at her in alarm. With her eyes tightly closed in ecstasy, her lips parted and an expression of other-worldly bliss on her face, she also looked, to say the least, a trifle unbalanced. Lopsided was the only word for it. California appeared to have suffered a major earthquake; Atlantic City had been pierced by a thin sliver of greenish glass to which a piece of label was still attached. Reaching down to remove it he became aware of a slow hiss of escaping air. He tried to push the glass back into place but it was too late. A deep depression was already settling over the area. As he braced himself for an explosion of wrath he noticed for the first time that her blouse was flecked with red.

'You are hurt?' Even as he spoke he realised that the blood was coming from a small cut to his chest.

Fräulein Brünnhilde uttered a low moan, waving her head from side to side. '*Mein Leibfraumilch!*' Her grip tightened. 'That was wonderful! The earth moved. Did you feel it? The earth moved.'

'Yes,' said Monsieur Pamplemousse cautiously. 'I felt it too.' All movement was relative. Speaking for himself he felt as if they were halfway to Evian.

'*Mein Beerenauslese!*' The breath was suddenly squeezed from his body as she tightened her grip. 'More! More!'

Monsieur Pamplemousse looked round for help but only Pommes Frites was there to answer his call. Pommes Frites averted his gaze. He was not without

**153**

his finer feelings. There would be no help from that quarter.

'Love is a very inexact science,' he gasped, playing for time as he tried to regain his breath before the next onslaught. 'It is like the boiling of an egg. Success cannot always be guaranteed. The joy of getting it exactly right is not always easy to repeat.'

Fräulein Brünnhilde gave another moan and a shudder went through her whole body as she relived the moment.

'*Mein Trockenbeerepauslese*. It has never happened to me before.'

'I doubt,' said Monsieur Pamplemousse, 'if it has ever happened to *anyone* quite like that before.'

'*Mein Eiswein* . . . please . . .'

Monsieur Pamplemousse tried to distract her. 'Eiswein is made from grapes which have been left hanging on the vine until after Christmas. They are picked while still frozen. The wine is sweet beyond measure, but it happens rarely. Perhaps once in a decade.'

Fräulein Brünnhilde opened her eyes. He noticed for the first time how blue they were. 'Then let it happen again. Please let it happen again.'

'It is not yet Christmas,' began Monsieur Pamplemousse.

'Neither am I cold.'

'Perhaps,' said Monsieur Pamplemousse, bowing to the inevitable, 'we may do a deal. There are ways in which you can help me. But first you must let me go so that I can move the car.'

Fräulein Brünnhilde closed her eyes again. 'Do not be long. I cannot bear it if you are too long.'

'I will be as quick as I can,' said Monsieur Pamplemousse. Struggling free, he clambered unsteadily to his feet, signalling to Pommes Frites as he did so.

Pommes Frites jumped up wagging his tail. He sensed there was some kind of game afoot. Pommes Frites liked games and this one promised to be even better than usual.

# 8
## A Meal to End All Meals

THE FIRST HALF OF THE JOURNEY BACK DOWN the mountain to the Institut des Beaux Arbres was conducted in silence. Pommes Frites spent most of the time gazing pensively out of the rear window, thinking thoughts, while casting superior glances at sheep grazing in the gathering dusk. Monsieur Pamplemousse was too busy concentrating on holding the 2CV in check with the handbrake to bother about making polite conversation. His mind was also racing on ahead to coming events. Now that he had marshalled his ideas he wanted to put them into action as quickly as possible. Speed was of the essence. Speed and confidence. Plus a reasonable amount of luck. The key to the Sanatorium was now safely in his pocket. He would have no hesitation whatsoever in using it. If necessary he would call in the local police. But that would involve lots of tedious explanations which would take time. Time was the one commodity he was short of. If all else failed, he would take it as high as he could possibly go. And if that failed . . . if that failed then at least he would have the satisfaction of knowing he had tried. His own conscience would be clear. Besides, he still had friends in the right *journaux*.

Fräulein Brünnhilde was busy with her thoughts too. 'Do you think the first time was best?' she asked suddenly. 'Or do you think the fourth?'

Monsieur Pamplemousse let go his concentration for a moment, long enough to glance across at her in wonder. She was like a child with a new toy, or a cat who had just discovered the existence of cream. It was a good job the cords attaching the groundsheet to the car had finally broken. They might still be at it.

'I think the third time was best.' He turned his attention back to the road.

'That is interesting,' she mused dreamily. 'I wonder why.'

Monsieur Pamplemousse didn't reply. It was not a moment to discuss practicalities. The simple answer was that food and wine after the second excursion had provided new energy to go with the second wind, and by then Pommes Frites had also got into the swing of things. Equally excited at having discovered a new joy in life, he hadn't even bothered to jump clear of the car. But by the time they set off on the fourth trip digestive tracts had begun to rebel, romance had flown out of the window.

'It was good that Pommes Frites had a puncture

157

outfit. I have never before met a dog with a puncture outfit.'

'He is never without.' Monsieur Pamplemousse pulled hard on the brake as they approached a steep bend. Lights from houses in the valley below them were beginning to appear.

'And a cylinder of compressed air. That, too, is unusual.'

'It is for his kennel. He has an inflatable kennel. We do a lot of travelling together and sometimes he has to sleep outside. In the hot weather he prefers it.'

'Ah! There cannot be many dogs with an inflatable kennel.'

'As far as I know,' said Monsieur Pamplemousse, 'he is the only one. I had it specially made.'

'I had my *soutien-gorge* specially made. I sent away for it. It is also unusual. Have you met one before?'

'Never,' said Monsieur Pamplemousse. He had read of them. They had enjoyed a brief vogue at one time, or so he had been told, but he had never actually encountered one at first hand so to speak. Now that he had he could see why they had never caught on. If he ever met one again he would treat it with respect, sticking to sea-level, where the air pressure was normal. As the road levelled out and they reached a comparatively straight section he took advantage of the moment to glance across at his companion again.

'It is not necessary. In your case it is far from necessary. It is like gilding the lily.'

He felt a hand on his knee. 'You are very kind.'

'I am only speaking the truth.'

'It is good for my ego. The *soutien-gorge*, I mean.'

'What is good for the ego is sometimes bad for

other things. Egos are like stomachs—they often grow too fat for comfort.'

Fräulein Brünnhilde looked down at herself. 'You think I should lose my egos?'

'I know you should. People are what they are. I have never met anyone yet who didn't want to change themselves in some way; a larger nose or a smaller one, or one which is straight, or to be thinner or fatter, or taller or shorter. And for what reason? It is like buying a book by a film star telling you how to become as beautiful as she is. It is pointless. If she thought for one moment that there was any possibility of it happening she would withdraw it from sale. Why should people always want to look like someone else? Everyone is different; that is part of the joy of life.'

'I shall keep them as a souvenir. You would like my egos as a souvenir?'

Monsieur Pamplemousse shook his head. 'It would not be a good idea. Madame Pamplemousse would not be pleased.'

'Ah!' Fräulein Brünnhilde fell silent again.

It would certainly not be a good idea. Doucette wouldn't be at all happy if she came across a pair of inflatable *doudounes* tucked away in his bottom drawer. Explanations would be tedious, prolonged and utterly unbelieved.

Again he felt a hand on his knee, lighter this time. 'I think Madame Pamplemousse is a very lucky person. Does she think she is a lucky person?'

Monsieur Pamplemousse weighed the question in his mind. It was hard to say. You could live with someone half a lifetime and still not know their true feelings.

'I cannot answer that,' he said at last. 'She looks forward to my coming home, that I know. But then, I think sometimes after a few days she looks forward to my going away again.'

'And you? Do you look forward to going home?'

'Yes. But then I also look forward to going away again. It is a good arrangement. We are not unhappy. It is the need to go back which is important. That, and the need to be wanted back.'

Another two corners and they were nearly there. As the perimeter fence came into view he pulled in to the side of the road and switched off the engine.

'Tell me.' Fräulein Brünnhilde took the photograph from her handbag and looked at it. 'Is it because you have no children that you are interested in this girl?'

Monsieur Pamplemousse considered the question carefully before replying. It was true in a way. Without his realising it and without ever having spoken to her, he felt he knew her and wanted to protect her. 'It is certainly not for the reason you might think.'

'That is all right then. I would not have liked that. I will help you.'

'Good.' He took the photograph from her. 'You know what to do?'

'Precisely.' She went over his instructions again.

'Excellent. You had better pack some things. Ask the girl to do the same. As for the other—we will work that out later.' He looked at his watch. It said 18.52. That it had survived the buffeting on the mountain was something of a miracle; a testimony to its makers—Capillard Rième. He might write to them. Except that it would be impossible to explain all that had actually happened. They would never be able to use it as advertising material.

'You had better check your own watch. I will be back here at 20.00 precisely.'

'I am sorry. My watch has stopped. It has 14.12.'

'In that case you had better borrow mine. I have my car clock. It is important that you are not late.'

He slipped the watch off his wrist and suddenly felt naked without it. Second only to his pen it was the personal possession he treasured most. As he slipped it over Fräulein Brünnhilde's wrist and began doing up the strap she gave a shiver.

'You are cold?'

'No. Suddenly a little lonely. That is all. After to-night I will not see you again.'

'If all goes well I will see you in Paris.'

'That will not be the same.'

No, it would not be the same. The cobbled streets of the Butte Montmartre would not lend themselves to such goings on. Doucette would be keeping a watchful eye on him as well.

'It is always unwise to try and go back; to repeat the unrepeatable.'

She gave a laugh. It was a good sign—the first time he had heard it. 'I have been thinking. I do not even know your name.'

'My friends call me Aristide.'

He felt the barest touch on his forehead; a butterfly of a kiss. Then the door opened.

'Thank you, Aristide. I shall leave my watch where it stopped. It will always remind me of a very happy afternoon in the mountains.'

He allowed her to walk a little way down the road before starting the engine, then caught up with her

**161**

just as she was disappearing through a gap in the bushes. He fielded the second kiss in mid-air and mimed putting it into his pocket, then she was gone.

Pommes Frites gave a loud yawn and began moving about restlessly on the back seat. Monsieur Pamplemousse took the hint and stopped for a moment to allow him into the front. It still felt warm from Fräulein Brünnhilde. A moment later they were on their way again, each busy with their own thoughts.

It was late when Monsieur Pamplemousse finally entered the dining-room of Les Cinq Parfaits. The tables were full; the ceremony of the raising of the domes was in full swing; there was a buzz of animated conversation.

He was walking somewhat stiffly; joints were beginning to seize up, muscles making their presence felt, rebelling against doing even the simplest of day-to-day tasks like moving his legs. Even a long, hot bath hadn't persuaded them to behave otherwise. He paused by the window separating the *cuisine* from the restaurant. The scene on the other side of the darkened glass was reminiscent of the performance of a modern ballet. The *commis-poissonnier* partnered Gilbert in a *pas-de-deux* over some *truite*, sprinkling almonds over it like confetti with all the masculine delicacy and authority of a Nureyev. The *commis-rotisseur* and Edouard were limbering up in front of an oven, preparing themselves for their own particular moment of truth. Alain was just disappearing offstage with a large bowl.

There was a new face where Jean-Claude would normally have been; perhaps the *commis-pâtissier* was enjoying his big moment as a stand-in. He glanced at his watch. By now Jean-Claude would be well on his way to Paris. All around the *cuisine* the *corps-de-ballet* moved swiftly and with precision, gathering up dishes with lightning speed, conveying them to the *sous-chef* for final inspection and checking before handing them over to the waiters and thence to the diners in the other room. Of Albert there was no sign. Turning round, he caught sight of a white hat at the far end of the restaurant. He must be doing his rounds.

Monsieur Pamplemousse made his way towards his table. It was the cue for action. Again, it was akin to a ballet. Waiters preceded him. Greetings were exchanged in the correct pecking order. His chair was moved back and carefully replaced, the moment judged to a nicety. The napkin was whisked away, shaken open and placed on his lap. He ordered an apéritif—a Kir made with *framboise;* the house speciality.

The menu materialised, along with a bottle of the ubiquitous Evian—one more out of the six hundred million which left the factory every year. The *carte des vins* was placed discreetly within his reach, a plate of hot *friandises* appeared on the table as if by magic—slivers of sausage encased in the lightest of pastry. He tried one; it positively melted in his mouth. Jean-Claude's stand-in was making the most of his opportunity. The cast withdrew, leaving him to his *friandises* and his ponderings on the evening's events.

Doucette had taken the news that she was about to be invaded remarkably well, entering into the situation with brisk efficiency. Rooms would be aired, beds would have to be remade. No doubt she would rush out and buy some flowers. There was no telling. Perhaps she'd sensed the urgency in his voice. Perhaps it was simply a need to feel wanted. As soon as he got back to Paris he would have to make other arrangements. Dinner accompanied by long, hot glances from Fräulein Brünnhilde would not go down well. There would be language barriers with the English girl. On the other hand, they might all get on like a house on fire. You never could tell.

First things first. He turned his attention to the menu. In all probability it would be his last meal at Les Cinq Parfaits. He must make the most of it. Tonight there would be no face at the window to spoil his appetite.

The whole operation at the Institut des Beaux Arbres had gone like a dream. In many ways it felt like a dream. Bluff had been the order of the day; borrowing the black boy who had shown him to Jean-Claude's room on the first evening, a happy thought. It had added the necessary stroke of realism. In the event Madame Schmidt had queried neither his sudden metamorphosis from being the emissary of a prospective student to that of a person of authority, nor the removal of Jean-Claude. Her husband had been more suspicious, asking for papers. He'd had to lean on him a little, adopting his long-practised 'I'm asking the questions' voice. 'Watch it, or it will be the worse for you.' It worked as it had always worked in the past. Pommes Frites had bared his teeth with great effect at the appropriate moment.

The taxi driver with his borrowed limousine had behaved magnificently; assuming exactly the right degree of studied indifference—of having seen it all before, leaning against the bonnet picking his teeth until required, his cap at a suitably insolent and rakish angle. He might have abducted people every day of his life. Perhaps he had in the past. The meeting with Fräulein Brünnhilde and the girl had gone without a hitch. Madame Grante would throw a fit when she saw the bill, but that was a minor problem.

A little way along the restaurant the V.I.P. was holding court. The table had been set very slightly and very discreetly apart from the rest. There were four other members of the entourage, each vying for the privilege of ministering to his wants; no doubt acting as bodyguards as well. He made a joke. Rolls of fat loosely encased in silken robes shook with laughter. It was echoed in turn by an obedient ripple round the table. Watching the scene over the top of his menu, Monsieur Pamplemousse couldn't help but wonder what would happen if one of them missed his cue. He wouldn't fancy their chances. What was it the chief had said about him?

'A *grosse légume* whose speed at acquiring untold wealth had not so far been matched by any show of finer feelings towards his fellow man.'

Behind the laughter there lurked corruption and decay. The black boy had said much the same on the journey up to the Institut. 'He make Idi Amin look like guardian angel on church outing.'

Even as he watched there occurred an incident which, although comparatively minor, served to underline the boy's words. One of the *commis*-waiters bearing a load of silver domes back to the kitchen passed perilously close to the great man's elbow and in swerving to avoid a collision inadvertently allowed one of them to fall to the floor.

165

The *Grosse Légume*, the flow of his conversation momentarily checked, half-rose and for a moment Monsieur Pamplemousse thought he was about to strike the waiter. The boy thought so too, and ducking in panic, he allowed the rest of the silverware to slide ignominiously off the tray.

The crash echoed round the room and for a moment there was a stunned silence. Then someone gave a nervous giggle in the way that people do in restaurants the world over at such moments and the tension was broken.

The *Grosse Légume* sat down again and a broad smile filled his face. But it was a smile without mirth and it left a long shadow. At another time and in another place, it seemed to say, your life would not be worth living. The man was a *salaud. Un salaud de première classe.*

'*Vous avez choisi, Monsieur?*' The maître d'hôtel appeared at his side, pad and pencil at the ready.

Monsieur Pamplemousse came down to earth. He had already decided against a repeat of the *menu gastronomique*. It would be like trying to recapture the delights of his experience on the mountainside. On the other hand it was an occasion for a mini-celebration of some kind. What would Holmes have chosen? Oysters and a brace of pheasants, probably, followed by cheddar cheese and syllabub. He corrected himself, the latter two courses would have been in the reverse order in the English manner. He scanned the menu. All four items were conspicuous by their absence.

Running his eye down the *entrées* he had a sudden thought. Amongst those listed he noticed a starred dish—*soupe aux truffes noires*—the one that Bocuse had created specially for President Giscard d'Estaing's famous *Légion d'Honneur* lunch at the Elysée Palace in 1975. He had always wanted to try it. He glanced across at the list of *poissons*. At the time, Bocuse had called on other chefs to contribute to the menu. Sure enough, the Troisgros Brothers' *escalope de saumon à l'oseille*—a creation based on a happy thought by Pierre Troisgros' mother-in-law, was also listed and starred. He felt a growing excitement. There were more delights—roast duck Claude Jolly. He remembered that in the original lunch they had followed duck with cheese, then the first wild strawberries of the year. Jean-Claude's *Soufflé Surprise* probably hadn't seen the light of day then—but he could make do with some more of the *framboises*.

The maître d'hôtel nodded approvingly. '*Monsieur* is not in a hurry?'

'I have nowhere to go,' said Monsieur Pamplemousse simply. 'I have all the time in the world.' It wasn't strictly true, of course. But tomorrow was another day.

He picked up his copy of *The Hound of the Baskervilles* and was about to open it where he'd left off, when Albert Parfait hobbled into view.

Monsieur Pamplemousse looked up at the slowly approaching figure with a genuine sense of shock. In the space of a few days the *patron* of Les Cinq Parfaits seemed to have added another ten years to his age. There was a stoop which he hadn't noticed previously, and his limp seemed more pronounced. But as he drew near he saw it was mostly in the eyes. The eyes were those of a man who had suddenly grown tired of life.

'What news?'

'Your son is safe.' Monsieur Pamplemousse felt a tremble in the other's hand as he took it, then the grip tightened.

'*Merci*. I was almost beginning to give up hope.'

'I'm sorry I didn't tell you straight away. Time did not allow it.'

Even as he spoke the words, Monsieur Pamplemousse knew that they had a hollow ring to them. It was an excuse rather than a reason. An excuse for an inexcusable omission. Deep down he had been avoiding the moment and he wondered why. It left him with a strange feeling; one which he couldn't entirely rationalise.

'I understand.' Albert Parfait relaxed momentarily, allowed himself a brief smile, then the tiredness returned to his face. It was almost as though he had been undergoing some kind of inner battle, the outcome of which had already been decided. 'When can I see him?'

'He is on his way to Paris for a few days. He has been heavily sedated, but he is young and fit—the effects will soon wear off. He will be back here as quickly as possible, but for the time being it is as well if he is not around.'

'And the girl?'

'The girl is travelling with him. She will be staying with Madame Pamplemousse. Pommes Frites is accompanying them on the journey. They will be quite safe.'

He didn't mention Fräulein Brünnhilde. It was unnecessary. There would be the girl's parents to tell too. His heart sank at the prospect.

'I am very grateful. Later tonight we will drink to

the occasion.' Once again there was a distinct tremble in the hand. 'In the meantime, I will leave you to your reading and to your meal. *Bon appetit.*'

Left to his own devices, Monsieur Pamplemousse picked up his book again and gazed at it unseeingly, focusing his thoughts not on the jumble of words but on the scene around him and on Albert Parfait in particular. He had a strange sense of foreboding. Monsieur Parfait did not look a happy man. The news of his son's safety had revived his spirits momentarily, but it had been only the briefest of moments. Perhaps he was suffering the responsibility of success and wealth. It must have been a difficult week for him. First the disappearance of Jean-Claude, then the arrival of the V.I.P., whose presence he could hardly have welcomed at such a time. It must be a far cry from the comparatively modest hopes and ambitions he'd nursed when he'd first helped out in his *grand-mère's* kitchen. He couldn't have dreamed in those far-off times that one day he would be hobnobbing with royalty, cooking for Presidents, playing host to the V.I.P.s of the world. All the same, it hardly accounted for his doom-laden manner.

Once again his thoughts were interrupted. This time by the wine waiter. He picked up the *carte des vins* and opted for a Hermitage—a bottle of Gérard Chave, one of the most meticulous of *vignerons*, whose land was so sheer the grape-filled *bennes* had to be hauled up to the top by a winch at harvest time.

Again his order met with evident approval. Then, having duly recorded it, the *sommelier* hovered for a moment, fingering his *tastevin* hesitantly. Clearly, he had something on his mind. Monsieur Pamplemousse raised his eyebrows enquiringly.

'I am sorry about the Château d'Yquem, *Monsieur*.'

'Sorry?' Monsieur Pamplemousse gazed at the man in amazement. 'But it was delicious. Sheer perfection. An unforgettable experience. I cannot wait to repeat it.'

'Ah!' A look of unhappiness crossed the *sommelier*'s normally dead-pan features. It was the kind of expression he must reserve for those rare occasions when he sniffed a cork and detected signs of the dreaded weevil bug. '*Monsieur* has not been to his refrigerator since this morning?'

Monsieur Pamplemousse thought for a moment. 'I have, but only briefly. I have been out all day.' It was true. He'd arrived back so late he'd even resisted the temptation of allowing himself the luxury of a drink with his bath. 'Why do you ask?'

'I am sorry, *Monsieur*. The room maid should have told you. On Monsieur Parfait's instructions we removed the second bottle. The wine should not have been withdrawn from the cellars in the first place.' He picked up the *carte des vins* and opened it at a page near the back. A neat red line had been drawn through one of the entries. 'As *Monsieur* will see, the '45 is no longer listed.'

Monsieur Pamplemousse digested the fact with mounting irritation.

'May I ask a simple question?'

'*Monsieur*?'

'If the '45 is no longer listed, then how was it that the night before last I was given two bottles when I ordered them. It was also my understanding that they were not the last.'

'There were three, *Monsieur*. Now there are only two. They were being held in reserve for a special customer. We will, of course, replace *Monsieur*'s second bottle with one from another year. Might I suggest the '62? *Monsieur* will not be charged.'

Monsieur Pamplemousse fixed the man with a stare. There were times when he would have dearly loved to announce his identity; hand over a card bearing the *escargot rampant*, symbol of *Le Guide*. 'I have another question. Would it not be true to say that in a restaurant such as Les Cinq Parfaits, a restaurant whose reputation is such that people come from all over the world to sample its *cuisine*, each and every guest should be considered special?'

'I agree, *Monsieur*, but unfortunately some guests like to be considered more special than others. It is the way of the world.' He allowed himself a brief glance at the table further along the room. 'We have to humour them.'

'Ah!' The penny dropped.

'He has a sweet tooth, *Monsieur*. The decision is not entirely ours.'

'*D'accord*. I understand.' It was the second time he'd heard mention of a 'sweet tooth'. The phrase was beginning to grate.

'*Merci, Monsieur*.' The *sommelier* made to leave. 'If *Monsieur* will forgive me?'

'Of course.'

Monsieur Pamplemousse drained his Kir, helped himself to the remaining *bonne bouche*, then sank back in his seat while he awaited the arrival of the first course. It might be the way of the world, but there were times when the ways of the world didn't suit him and this was one of them. In truth, the chance to compare the '62 Château d'Yquem with its illustrious predecessor would not be without interest—he could hardly grumble. It was the principle, or lack of it, which irritated.

Another ripple of laughter from the offending party did nothing to improve his mood. At least they were approaching the end of their meal. The cheese trolley had been and gone, the table cleared in readiness for the next course. He wondered what kind of reception would be accorded the *Soufflé Surprise*. No doubt, to add to his feeling of injustice, it would be washed down with 'his' wine. He resolved to look the other way.

Seeing a flotilla of waiters approaching, their leader bearing a silver tray on which reposed the inevitable dome, he poured himself a glass of Evian and hastily cleansed his palate in readiness. At the same moment, through another door, the *sommelier* reappeared with his wine, reaching the table a moment before the others. The bottle presented, it was discreetly removed to a side table for opening and decanting. He sat up, preparing himself for the moment of truth, taste-buds springing to life with anticipation.

The junior waiters stood back in attitudes of suitable reverence as the plate was placed in front of him and the dome removed, revealing a deep earthenware bowl capped and sealed with a mound of golden pastry, puffed up like a gigantic mushroom.

Picking up a spoon, he pierced the top, breaking the flakes into small pieces so that they fell back into the bowl and released the smell. It was rich and woody, like nothing he had ever encountered before. A complex mixture; the result of combining a *matignon* of carrots, celery, onions, mushrooms, and unsalted butter with chicken *consommé*, *foie gras* and fresh truffles. A unique creation. No wonder Bocuse had been awarded the *Légion d'Honneur*. No wonder Monsieur Parfait spent so much on truffles every year. Both were fully justified.

He tasted the wine. Like the soup, it had been made with love. It was a perfect marriage. Automatically he reached for the notebook he always carried concealed in his right trouser leg and laid it on his lap, out of sight below the edge of the tablecloth. It was an occasion to record; one which would have met with Pommes Frites' wholehearted approval. He felt a momentary pang of guilt as he caught sight of the time on his watch. It was just after ten o'clock. By now Pommes Frites would have reached the *autoroute*, speeding on his supperless way to Paris. He made a mental note to ring Doucette as soon as dinner was over and remind her to put something out in readiness for his arrival.

He leant over the bowl again. Whoever said that the *bouquet* was often better than the taste would have had to eat not only his words, but the most heavenly dish imaginable. Spoon halfway to his mouth, he paused yet again in order to savour the deliciousness of the smell, and as he did so a frown came over his face. Heading in his direction was one of the page-boys, holding aloft yet another silver tray. He watched as the boy threaded his way in and out of the tables. What was it now?

He eyed a small sheaf of papers gloomily and, stifling his feelings, motioned for them to be left beside him. It was hardly the boy's fault. He was only doing as he'd been told. It was more his own fault for not having called in at the reception desk for so long.

Another spoonful of soup and he succumbed to temptation. There was a card from Doucette—a drawing of the Sacré Coeur—reminding him of someone's birthday. He couldn't make out the words in the muted lighting. Never mind, he would work it out later.

The thought occurred to him that Pommes Frites might be good at hunting truffles. He had a nose for scents. Truffles might be just up his street. The *'egregious tuberculum'* as Brillet-Savarin had called them; 'a luxury of kept women'. Perhaps one day, if they found themselves in Périgord . . .

There was a telex from the Director. The one he had spoken of on the telephone. Short and to the point, it said: CANCEL ORDER FOR *SOUFFLÉ SURPRISE* IMMEDIATELY. The girl in charge of the telex machine at Les Cinq Parfaits must be wondering what was going on. He hoped she hadn't relayed it to the kitchen first by mistake.

He picked up the envelope and opened it. It was a letter from Durelle. He skimmed through it quickly, then stopped halfway and began reading it again, much more slowly this time.

*Merde!* It was not possible.

His *soupe aux truffes noires* momentarily forgotten, Monsieur Pamplemousse read through the letter for a third time, still hardly able to believe his eyes.

'Aristide, you old *maquereau!*' it ran. 'How did you know it was my fiftieth birthday? You really had me fooled. When your bottle arrived and I saw the label I thought it's Aristide up to his tricks again. Trust Aristide to think of putting Pommes Frites' specimen into a bottle labelled Château d'Yquem '45. I even took it into the lab for analysis. Then when I opened it and discovered the truth I could hardly believe my eyes. Such wine! It was out of this world! If I had known I would have waited until you got back to Paris so that we could share it. I don't know what I have done to deserve such riches, let alone how I can ever thank you, but I am working on the problem. Your friend, Raymonde.'

*Sapristi!* He didn't believe it. It had to be some kind of a joke.

Picking up Doucette's card he held it up to the candle and reread the message on the back. The words confirmed what Durelle had said. It had been his fiftieth birthday.

He sat back in order to collect his scattered thoughts. He knew that he had taken the right bottle from the refrigerator. Or rather, to be pedantic (not to say Holmesian) about it, he knew he had taken the one which he'd thought was the correct bottle, simply because it was where he had put it the night before. In his haste he hadn't examined it closely. The answer must be that in checking the contents, something she would do every morning as a matter of routine in order to see what had been consumed, the room maid must have inadvertently swapped the bottles over.

A second, more sobering thought struck him; one which caused a slow smile to spread across his face as it sank in. If Durelle had been sent a genuine bottle of the '45, then Pommes Frites' sample must have gone back into stock when the second bottle was withdrawn. And if it had gone back into stock and there was only one other bottle left, then it was a fifty-fifty chance it would arrive in the restaurant at any moment.

Monsieur Pamplemousse's smile grew wider. It would be rough justice if it did. He couldn't think of a more suitable recipient than the odious character at present holding court. His only regret was that Pommes Frites wouldn't be there to witness the event.

Polishing off the remains of his soup, he dabbed at his mouth with a napkin, then leaned back in his chair, anxious not to miss a single moment. Mathematically it might not happen, but if there was any justice in the world then mathematics would fly out of the window.

He wasn't a moment too soon. He had hardly settled himself before the *sommelier* appeared. Carrying a cradled bottle reverentially in both hands, he made his way across the dining-room towards the V.I.P.'s table. The formalities completed, the bottle presented and inspected, the label read and its inscription confirmed, he stood back and reached into his apron pocket for a corkscrew while those around the table voiced appreciation of their host's impeccably good taste.

Monsieur Pamplemousse's face fell again. He wished now he'd paid more attention to the remains of the soup instead of bolting it down without a moment's thought. He'd been living in cloud-cuckoo-land. Even if the bottle did turn out to be the one containing Pommes Frites' specimen, it wouldn't get any further than the opening. One sniff of the cork would reveal all; the other bottle would be sent for immediately. On reflection, it was just as well. The scandal if it turned out that Les Cinq Parfaits had served *pipi de chien* to one of the guests in mistake for a Château d'Yquem would reverberate around the restaurants of France for years.

Idly he watched the beginnings of a set and invariable routine he'd seen countless times before; the application of the corkscrew, its deft rotation, the swift but sure single leverage ensuring the clean removal of the cork, the passing of it under the nose . . .

Suddenly he sat up and leaned across the table, concentrating all his attention on the scene in front of him. Before the *sommelier* had a chance to complete his task, almost before the cork had left the bottle, Albert Parfait appeared at his side. There was a brief exchange of words and then Monsieur Parfait himself took over, removing the cork from the screw and slipping it straight into the pocket of his apron without so much as a second glance.

Monsieur Pamplemousse's eyes narrowed as a thought entered his mind and then emerged almost immediately as an inescapable conclusion. It could only mean one of two things; either the *patron* didn't trust his *sommelier* before such important guests, or there was something about the bottle of wine which might cause the V.I.P. to reject it. The former was so unlikely that he dismissed it, allowing his mind to race on ahead as he watched the wine being poured into a glass ready for tasting.

Unable to stand it a moment longer, Monsieur Pamplemousse snapped his notebook shut and sprang to his feet. A joke was a joke, but he couldn't allow it to happen. He *must* not allow it to happen. More than that, the evidence had to be destroyed. Albert Parfait was an idiot. Not only was the honour of Les Cinq Parfaits at stake, but also that of *Le Guide,* its contemporaries, even that of France itself.

Ignoring those around him, his stiffness forgotten,

scattering the waiters as he went, Monsieur Pample-mousse reached the table in a matter of seconds and removed the offending glass from Albert Parfait's hand, placing it on a side table out of reach of the diners.

Their eyes met briefly. Failure was written large on Albert's face; failure and something else. Despera-tion? A mute cry for help? Whatever it was there could be no time for speculation.

Before anyone had a chance to react, Monsieur Pamplemousse whisked the bottle from its cradle and upended it into a nearby plant container. The effect of his action was both immediate and impressive. He stared at the plant. Its leaves were turning yellow and wilting before his very eyes.

Marvelling at the potency of Pommes Frites' water, he turned towards the *Grosse Légume* and braced himself for the inevitable explosion. But hardly had he done so than there was a new diversion. Aware of a movement from behind, a movement which was followed almost immediately by a choking sound, Mon-sieur Pamplemousse spun round on his heels and was just in time to see a hand clutching an empty glass disappear from view on the other side of the table.

Attention, which a moment before had been fo-cused in his direction, suddenly switched as glass and silverware and china crashed to the floor, over-riding the dull thud which preceded it.

As those nearby craned their necks in alarm, an elderly man jumped to his feet and rushed to the rescue, bending over the figure on the floor with a professional air.

Monsieur Pamplemousse hurried round the table to join him. 'I think, *Monsieur*,' he murmured as he crouched, 'you will find it is only a temporary indisposition. The most it will require is the use of a stomach pump.'

The man looked up at him. 'On the contrary, *Monsieur*. I am a doctor and I think you will find on closer examination that Monsieur Parfait is beyond such aids. Monsieur Parfait, alas, is en route to the *grande cuisine* in the sky.'

# 9

## APÉRTIFS WITH MADAME GRANTE

'PAMPLEMOUSSE.' THE DIRECTOR HELD A SHEAF of papers above his desk; heavily embossed notepaper, pink flimsies, yellow duplicates, sheets of memo paper. 'Congratulations are being showered upon you. They arrive by the hour. I trust I may add mine?' He released his grip and they fluttered down at varying speeds, like multi-coloured leaves in an autumn breeze.

Monsieur Pamplemousse inclined his head non-committally, but warily.

The Director salvaged one of the heavier pieces of paper. 'This one is from the Minister himself. He would like to see you later today—at your convenience. Word has also reached me from the Elysée Palace. Your name has been recorded. Even the *Grosse Légume* has let it be known that he wishes to honour you with a decoration—the Grand Order of the Star of something or other. It is accompanied by an invitation to become his chief food taster.'

Monsieur Pamplemousse shuddered.

'It carries a large salary commensurate with the post. The supply of wines would be without limit; the choice would be yours. Doubtless other pleasures would be at your command.'

'I think not, *Monsieur*.'

The Director breathed a visible sigh of relief. 'We would miss you, Aristide. The appointment is pensionable, but I doubt if you would live to enjoy it. You would also have suffered opprobrium from on high. Relations between our two countries are somewhat strained at present.'

'He has left France, *Monsieur*?'

'At the highest possible speed. He and his entire entourage flew out last night on a specially chartered plane. The visit to Les Beaux Arbres has been postponed indefinitely. Outwardly he took diplomatic umbrage, but in reality he is a very frightened man. Like all bullies he is a coward at heart.

'The soil in the pot-plant container at Les Cinq Parfaits is undergoing analysis. Preliminary reports suggest that there was enough poison in the bottle to kill a regiment. Whoever put it there was determined to make a good job of it.'

Monsieur Pamplemousse leant down and gave Pommes Frites' ear an affectionate tweak. At least his worst fear hadn't been realised. Responsibility for the contents of the bottle of Château d'Yquem rested elsewhere. He gave another half-suppressed shudder as the thought crossed his mind that he might well have tested the wine himself had he not been in such a hurry.

'One almost regrets your act, Pamplemousse. I realise it was done with the best of intentions, but had the poison reached the person for whom it was intended few tears would have been shed. As it is, the world of *haute cuisine* has been deprived of one of its most revered figures. The loss will be severe. It was a most unfortunate accident.'

'Accident?' Monsieur Pamplemousse closed his eyes for a brief moment while he pictured the scene in the restaurant. Albert Parfait's appearance that evening—the haunted look in his eyes; the final air of desperation. 'I do not think it was an accident, *Monsieur*.'

'What are you suggesting, Pamplemousse? If it was not an accident, then . . .'

'I am convinced he knew what the bottle contained. That was why he took over its serving, and that being so, one can only assume the drinking of it to have been a deliberate and final act on his part.'

'Surely not. By then, according to your own account, he knew his son was safe. The *Grosse Légume* would soon be gone. He had everything to live for.'

'Perhaps, *Monsieur*, "had" is the right word.'

'Elucidate, Pamplemousse.'

Resisting the very real temptation to say, 'Elementary, my dear Watson', Monsieur Pamplemousse racked his brains for the right words. Dishonour? Shame? Disgrace? Failure? Albert Parfait had probably known more of what was going on than most. If he'd known what the bottle contained then he must have been a party to its preparation, if only at arm's length. No doubt, pressure had been brought to bear: pressure from faceless people in authority whose names would never be known, leaving him to face the music. He must have seen the writing on the wall. He was no fool.

'I think he could see ruination staring him in the face. Not financial ruin. People would still flock to Les Cinq Parfaits whatever happened. What he couldn't face was the loss of all the things for which he had worked so hard during his life; the things he knew would have made both his mother and his grandmother proud. He couldn't bear the thought of losing face where it mattered most. His Stock Pots in *Le Guide*, his stars in Michelin, his toques in Gault Millau.'

'You think it would have come to that?'

'Michelin never award a third star to a restaurant simply for the food alone,' said Monsieur Pamplemousse. 'Nor, *Monsieur,* do we award our Stock Pots for that reason. The withdrawal might only have been temporary, but they would have been withdrawn and he couldn't face the thought.'

It was the Director's turn to fall silent. It had happened before, of course. There had been the famous occasion when a chef had committed suicide because of the loss of his only star in Michelin.

'Ours is a heavy responsibility, Aristide,' he said at last. 'The irony is that Les Cinq Parfaits will lose them anyway by virtue of Albert Parfait's own act.'

'Only if the act is made public, *Monsieur.*'

The Director gave a start. 'What are you suggesting, Pamplemousse?'

'I am suggesting that if Albert Parfait's death is put down to heart failure—which covers a multitude of sins—then things will go on as before.'

'I am afraid that is not possible. I cannot agree. Knowing what I know, my conscience would not allow it.'

'In that case,' Monsieur Pamplemousse felt inside

his jacket pocket and withdrew a folded sheet of paper. 'I am afraid, *Monsieur,* I have to tender my resignation. My own conscience would not allow me to continue.' It was the least he could do. The mental picture of Albert Parfait's last imploring look remained vividly in his mind. A cry for help if ever he'd seen one. A cry that he'd unwittingly ignored.

The Director took the sheet of paper and stared at it disbelievingly. 'What if I refuse to accept it?'

'That is your decision, *Monsieur.* I shall be elsewhere.'

'You realise what you are asking, Aristide?'

'If it is possible to hush up the business of the Institut,' said Monsieur Pamplemousse, 'as I am sure it will be, then doubtless it will also be possible to hush up the cause of Albert Parfait's death. Publication of the facts will do no one any good. Representations in certain quarters . . . a word in the right ear . . . I am sure you have many contacts, *Monsieur* . . .'

There was a long pause. 'And if I do? Will you allow me to tear up this ridiculous letter?'

'Perhaps,' said Monsieur Pamplemousse stubbornly. 'We shall have to wait and see. Jean-Claude will take over.'

'He knows about his father?'

Monsieur Pamplemousse nodded. 'I broke the news to him this morning.'

'How has he taken it?'

'It was a shock, although he had been expecting something to happen. It was the way it happened that bothered him most.'

'You think he is capable of becoming *patron*?'

'I am sure of it, *Monsieur.* It was his father's wish. He will rise to the occasion. Besides, he will not be alone. He will have the support of his brothers.' He took out his wallet and removed the photograph of the girl. 'He also has someone to work for and if all goes well, to help him. They have already been through a lot together.'

The Director took the photograph and studied it carefully.

'It was for her that Jean-Claude conceived his plan,' continued Monsieur Pamplemousse.

'She is very attractive, I agree. But why her? There must have been many such girls at the Institut.'

'When you are in love, *Monsieur*, it is always with the most beautiful girl in the world and always you fear for the attention of others. Jean-Claude knew the annual visit of the *Grosse Légume* was drawing near and he became more and more convinced that she would be amongst his targets. But short of abduction, he couldn't think of any good reason for getting her out of the way without bringing trouble on Les Cinq Parfaits. He needed something which would bring her parents running to her rescue without actually giving the game away. That was when he dreamed up the idea of the kidnap note and why it had to be in English. The timing was critical—it had to be immediately before the "visit". Unfortunately, just as he was about to put his plan into action something went wrong. Somehow or other, others got wind of it and panic set in. Getting rid of him for good was out of the question—he was too well known. Putting him out of action for a while in the Sanatorium was at best a temporary measure to keep him quiet while they tried to think what to do next.'

'I am curious to know what led you to the Institut so quickly,' broke in the Director. 'Locally, of course, I gather there had long been rumours about the place, but here in Paris there was nothing to connect it with Jean-Claude's disappearance. It was put down to all manner of things. At one point it was even suggested it might be the work of a foreign power. When you started your investigations on the instructions of certain people in authority, others started to panic. It had always been a case of the left hand not knowing what the right hand was doing. Orders were issued and then, as new facts came to light, promptly countermanded.'

Monsieur Pamplemousse gripped the arms of his chair impatiently. '*I* am curious to know how such a situation could ever have been allowed to develop in the first place. I find it incredible.'

'Ssh! Aristide!' Putting a finger to his lips, the Director got up from behind his desk, crossed to the door, opened it and having looked out to make sure the coast was clear, indicated to his secretary that they were not to be disturbed.

Back at his desk he settled down again and made nervous play with a set of large ball-bearings suspended from a kind of stainless steel trapeze. In the silence of the office it sounded like the opening day of the National Boules Championship.

'Politics, Aristide,' he said at last, 'is a dirty game. In this case what probably began as a tiny favour on someone's part, a greasing of the wheels in return for a consideration, escalated beyond anything that had been contemplated. Greed is a very powerful incentive, and so is security. People who have grown accustomed to their creature comforts will often do anything within their power to avoid losing them. It begins in the cradle. Try taking a rattle away from a baby and see what happens. Instinctively the grip tightens.

'The situation a few years ago when Europe—the whole of the Western world—suddenly found itself short of oil was very different to what it is now. We had grown accustomed to turning on the heat whenever we felt cold. Hot water poured from our taps. Engineers designed bigger and better cars powered by fuel which gushed out of our petrol pumps. It was there. It would always be there.

'When all that suddenly disappeared for a brief while there was panic. Queues formed at garages. In America men were shot for the sake of a gallon of *essence*. People began to hoard coal and oil. Orders went out to take immediate action. Those we wouldn't normally have been seen dead with were suddenly courted as friends. Nothing was too much trouble for them.

'No doubt when the *Grosse Légume* first came on the scene instructions were issued by someone, somewhere, that he was to receive the very best of treatment. Doors would be opened; his every wish pandered to. And when he expressed an interest in food, what better place to send him to than Les Cinq Parfaits? If the Parfaits objected, so much the worse for them. Bureaucracy wields a very heavy bludgeon when it comes to the renewal of licences. It also moves very slowly and is resistant to change. Those original orders were never rescinded.'

'And when the *Grosse Légume* expressed an interest in the pupils at the Institut des Beaux Arbres?' Monsieur Pamplemousse remained coldly unhelpful. 'Did bureaucracy again turn a blind eye?'

The Director gave a sigh. 'Different people have different standards, Aristide.'

He stood up and crossed to the window, gazing down at the slate-grey rooftops of the seventh arrondissement. To the right lay the Hôtel des Invalides, to the left the huge mass of the Eiffel Tower; on the hill beyond, the white confection of the Sacré Coeur stood out in the sunlight.

'Two and a half million people are at work out there. At work and at play, engaged in the sheer business of living. In the Ile de France ten million. In the whole of France, over fifty-three million. Men, women, old people, children, babies; French, Moroccans, Algerians, Portuguese; Catholics, Jews, Protestants, Moslems. Perhaps, for those who were involved at the time, those who had been charged with the task of humouring the whims of the *Grosse Légume*, there was no choice—the scales were too heavily weighted in his favour; fifty-three million to one. Perhaps in the beginning it was a simple case of minor corruption. We shall probably never know.'

'It does not excuse it, *Monsieur*,' said Monsieur Pamplemousse stubbornly.

'No, Aristide.' The Director turned away from the window. 'It does not excuse it. It merely explains it. I do not agree, nor do I entirely disagree. I was not in the position of having to make a decision. It is like asking someone if they approve or disapprove of transplanting the heart of a baboon into a child. If it is someone else's child they will most likely get hot under the collar and say no. If it is their own child the chances are they will say yes. It was probably an on-the-spot decision, and once that decision had been made there was no going back.'

'A wrong does not easily become a right, *Monsieur*. Two, still less. There were many wrongs to follow. Nine at the last count.'

The Director shrugged. 'The second time was that much easier, the third probably a matter of little moment. By then it would have become a game; a matter of mechanics. The Department of Dirty Tricks were called in to help, and to them it was an exercise, a chance to flex their muscles and to pit their wits against others—it didn't really matter who—they do not have their title for nothing. The school was taken over; the original ski instructors replaced by their own men; the *Grosse Légume* made a patron. His visits to both Les Cinq Parfaits and the Institut des Beaux Arbres became annual events; a chance to restock his larder, so to speak. He has, as you probably gathered, a very sweet tooth; plus a taste for blondes, preferably young and Anglo-Saxon. He likes their fresh complexions and they are more docile than some of the Latin races. At the Institut he was guaranteed an inexhaustible supply.'

'Why did he not go to Britain in that case?'

'Have you ever tried to smuggle a schoolgirl through the British Customs, Pamplemousse? They are not noted for their sympathetic approach to such matters. Besides, it is a small island. They lack certain of our advantages; space, mountains, borders . . . It was very much simpler to get them over here first, and the very fact of their being away from home had many other advantages.'

Monsieur Pamplemousse sat in silence for a moment or two. Reaching down with his hand he sought solace in the warmth and comfort of Pommes Frites' left ear. He suddenly felt very tired and dispirited and for no particular reason he thought again of Albert Parfait. That made him even sadder.

'And the radiators of France, *Monsieur*? What of them?'

The Director eyed Monsieur Pamplemousse uneasily. He sensed from his tone of voice the need to tread a delicate line. 'That is not for me to comment on, Aristide. No doubt the Minister responsible will have more to say on the subject when he sees you. It is, in any case, a rapidly changing situation. I am told that by 1990, seventy per cent of all our energy will come from nuclear sources. We are rich in hydro-electric power. Beneath the Pyrénées near Pau lies the largest deposit of natural gas on the continent of Europe waiting to be tapped. Solar energy is already being harnessed and fed into our National Grid. Each year there is less and less need to pander to the *grosses légumes* of this world.'

'And in the meantime, *Monsieur*?'

'In the meantime, Pamplemousse, we must hope for mild winters. What has happened is over and done with. Life doesn't stand still. Tomorrow's problems are already waiting in the wings. The *Grosse Légume* will have to do his "shopping" elsewhere in future. In France he is *persona non grata*. Such a situation will not be allowed to occur again.'

'And what about his past shopping?'

'Moves are being made; pressures exerted behind the scenes. The government will not be idle.'

'And what will happen to the Institut des Beaux Arbres?'

'Questions, Pamplemousse, questions. I think you will find that as from today the Institut is "under new management". The "ski instructors" will be replaced by the genuine article. Its pupils will remain untarnished—at least until they go out into the world.'

The Director waved aside the problems. They were for others to solve. 'You still haven't answered *my* question. What led you there in the first place?'

Monsieur Pamplemousse considered the matter carefully before replying. Luck, he supposed. Luck, and a certain amount of tedious spadework. Attention to detail. He would like to have added a touch of Holmesian deduction, but it had been more a matter of being in the right place at the right time, as was so often the case. Plus, of course, Pommes Frites' temporary indisposition.

The Director glanced down at the huge bulk beside Monsieur Pamplemousse's chair. 'I trust he is fully recovered?'

'*Absolument, Monsieur.*' Pommes Frites' breakfast that morning had been of gargantuan proportions. He'd had a lot of catching up to do. 'Had I not gone in search of him I would not have encountered the *doudounes.*'

'Ah, yes, the *doudounes.*' The Director perked up. 'I must say your red herring about looking for an illiterate female compositor with large *doudounes* was a masterly stroke, Pamplemousse. It had us all fooled. As a means of diverting attention away from your own activities it worked like a dream. Here at Headquarters, people were running around in ever-decreasing circles. Lists were compiled; descriptions circulated. The print unions were consulted; Interpol alerted. A photokit picture was painstakingly constructed, built up from the brief details at our disposal.' He reached down and opened one of his desk drawers. 'What do you think of this, Aristide?'

Monsieur Pamplemousse took a 20 x 25cm print from the Director and held it up to the light. The face looking back at him bore little resemblance to Fraülein Brünnhilde. She would not be at all pleased if she saw it. As for the rest—someone had had a field day.

'I would not like to meet such a person on a dark night, *Monsieur*,' he said.

The Director held out his hand. 'Blown up out of all proportion, eh, Pamplemousse?' Pleased with his own joke, he replaced the photograph in his desk drawer.

For a moment Monsieur Pamplemousse was tempted to say more, but only for a moment. A promise was a promise. That apart, he had a feeling it would provoke snide references to past cases; the *affaire* at La Langoustine involving Madame Sophie and the *gonflables* in particular. He could almost hear the Director's comments. 'There are those who would say you are developing a distressing penchant for inflatables, Pamplemousse. Were you by any chance frightened by some balloons when you were small?'

Outside, a clock began to chime. They both looked at their watches automatically. It was mid-day.

'There is a lot to digest, Aristide.' The Director reached for his telephone. 'I hope you don't mind, but I have asked Madame Grante to join us for a pre-*déjeuner* apéritif.'

Monsieur Pamplemousse's heart sank. 'Is that strictly necessary, *Monsieur*? I can explain the second dent in the other wing. As for the picnic, I agree it was somewhat elaborate, but there were good reasons . . .'

'The *second* dent, Pamplemousse?' The Director put his hand over the receiver. 'It must have been a very wide road sign.'

'I had another encounter, *Monsieur*. With a tree. Were he able to talk, Pommes Frites would bear witness that I was not to blame.'

'Ah!' It was hard to tell from the tone of the Director's voice whether he was registering understanding or resignation. A pained look came over his face. 'No, no, Madame Grante. It is not necessary to bring the appropriate forms with you. It can all be gone into later. This is a purely social occasion.'

'It seemed like a good idea at the time,' he said with a sigh as he replaced the receiver. 'She is not a bad woman and she has a difficult job to do. I sometimes feel, Aristide, that she labours under the impression that while she is slaving away at her desk all day others like yourself are living a sybaritic life out in the field.'

'A gross misapprehension, *Monsieur*.'

The Director rose to his feet and crossed the room to a cupboard at the far end immediately below the portrait of *Le Guide*'s founder, Hippolyte Duval. 'I know that, Pamplemousse. You know it. But given the size of your present claims, claims that I am sure can be fully justified in the fullness of time, I feel a little P.R. would not come amiss.' Opening the door of a concealed refrigerator he withdrew a bottle.

Monsieur Pamplemousse gazed at it in awe. Even from the other side of the room the contents were immediately recognisable.

'Taste-buds on the alert as ever, Aristide!' The Director looked pleased. 'I have not forgotten my promise. It is the Château d'Yquem '45.' Placing the bottle carefully on the cupboard top, he unfolded a white napkin and made ready a corkscrew and three tulip-shaped glasses. 'It is a long time since I last tasted it.'

Holding the glasses up to the light in turn to make sure they were scrupulously clean, he felt the bottle again. 'I hope it is not too cold.'

A knock at the door heralded the arrival of Madame Grante. In response to the Director's bidding she entered and gazed around the room, registering in one brief, all-embracing glance both its occupants and the array of drinking implements on the cupboard top. She bestowed on the former a thin-lipped, wintry smile. It was not, reflected Monsieur Pamplemousse, the kind of smile that would have raised the temperature of the wine had it been pointed in that direction; rather the reverse. Pommes Frites opened one eye and finding it greeted by a disapproving sniff, hurriedly closed it again.

'Ah, Madame Grante! How good to see you.' The Director's attempt to inject a note of *bonhomie* into the proceedings was not entirely successful. Nervousness was apparent in his voice. 'Please sit down and make yourself comfortable. I was just saying to Aristide that it is time we saw more of you.'

Madame Grante seated herself on a long, black leather couch near the door, straightening her skirt automatically as she did so. 'I am always available, *Monsieur*.'

She watched while the Director removed the cork from the bottle and began pouring the wine. 'Only a very small glass, *Monsieur*. Some of us do have to go back to work, you know.' The shaft, directed at Monsieur Pamplemousse, met with an unreceptive target. Turning back to the Director, she unbent a little. 'Unlike you hardened drinkers, I have to take care. One glass and I am not always accountable.' It was a joke she clearly kept for festive occasions—probably at office birthday parties and Christmas, and although it went unremarked by the other occupants of the room, it did not go unnoticed.

The Director looked even more nervous as he approached her, holding one of the glasses delicately by its stem. His eyes, as they met those of Monsieur Pamplemousse, clearly gave the green light for the other to take charge should the occasion demand it. As with Madame Grante's arrow, it fell on stony ground.

The second glass of wine deposited on a table beside Monsieur Pamplemousse's chair, the Director seated himself behind his desk again. He held his own glass up to the light and uttered a deep sigh of contentment.

'Ah, such depth of colour, such bliss . . . it makes one feel good to be alive.'

'It looks very expensive,' said Madame Grante disapprovingly.

'My dear lady'—the Director sounded put out—'of course it is expensive. Such wine can never be cheap. Grapes, infected by the "noble rot", are left on the vines to shrivel until they lose half their weight and are barely recognisable. Often they have to be painstakingly picked one by one; but the juice is lush and concentrated, rich in sugar and glycerine. Even then it is no easy matter. The wine is kept for three and a half years in cask, topped up twice a week . . . the result is overpowering—you can almost feel the weight.'

Seeing that Madame Grante remained unconvinced he swirled the contents round. 'Look at it. Note the deep, rich amber-gold. It is a luscious wine. It is like drinking a mixture of honey and *crème brûlée*. Would you say *crème brûlée*, Aristide?'

'It is an apt simile, *Monsieur*.'

'As for the bouquet . . . that is something else again . . .'

Raising the glass to his nose, the Director held it there for a brief moment while he inhaled deeply. '*Sacré bleu!*' The glass fell from his nerveless hand as he jumped to his feet. '*Mon Dieu! Nom d'un nom!* Have you smelt it, Pamplemousse?'

Monsieur Pamplemousse reached for his own glass, but before he had time to put it to the test there was a choking sound from the direction of the door. Looking round, he was just in time to see Madame Grante, a handkerchief already to her mouth, disappear through the opening. The slam as the door swung shut was echoed seconds later by another.

Pommes Frites, wakened by the commotion, rose to his feet. He peered at the half-empty glass on the table, gave it a proprietorial sniff, then stared at his master in surprise.

Avoiding his gaze, Monsieur Pamplemousse looked the Director straight in the eye. 'Did you say you *bought* this wine, *Monsieur*?'

'No, Pamplemousse, I did not say that. I made no mention of where it came from.' The Director sounded irritated. His voice was defensive. 'It was, as a matter of fact, a gift from Les Cinq Parfaits. It arrived this morning and I am told it was their last bottle. It seemed only right that you should share it.' He picked up his glass again and eyed the contents dubiously. 'What do you think can have happened to it? You have a nose for these things.'

'I think it is a little over the top, *Monsieur*.'

'A little over the top? It is *incroyable*. I have never smelt anything like it. It reminds me of that old *pissoir* near the Métro.'

'An even apter simile, *Monsieur.*' Monsieur Pample-mousse crossed to the cupboard and picked up the bottle. 'Perhaps the journey has unsettled it.'

'You think we should give it time?'

Monsieur Pamplemousse looked round the room. 'I think, *Monsieur,* it is yet another bottle destined for the pot plant.'

The Director watched unhappily while Monsieur Pamplemousse performed the task. 'This is becoming a habit, Pamplemousse.'

'At least Madame Grante will appreciate that life in the field is not all roses.'

The Director chuckled. 'She will not be querying your P39s for some while to come. Do you think she is all right?'

'I think she will recover.' Monsieur Pamplemousse decided against any further explanations. He'd had quite enough for one morning.

The Director joined him at the cupboard. 'Shall I open something else? I have a Beaumes-de-Venise. I am told that locally they drink it as an apéritif.'

Monsieur Pamplemousse shook his head. 'If you will forgive me, *Monsieur,* I must go. I have to get back to Montmartre. I may watch a little *boules* on the way while Pommes Frites enjoys the fresh air. I must not be late. Despite his troubles Jean-Claude has promised to prepare a *Soufflé Surprise.* Madame Pamplemousse is taking his mind off things in the kitchen.'

'I admire your stamina, Pamplemousse. I must say I have been quite put off my *déjeuner.* Besides . . .' The Director hesitated. 'I have another matter to deal with. One which requires a certain amount of deli-cacy in its handling. A complaint has been lodged.'

'A complaint, *Monsieur*?'

'Yes, Pamplemousse, a complaint. You are exercised by what happened at the Institut des Beaux Arbres. I am exercised about something that happened at Les Cinq Parfaits on the night of your arrival. It seems that one of the advance guard—a lesser wife of the *Grosse Légume*, mother, nevertheless, of twins—was attacked by a fetishist of the very worst kind. A fetishist whose bizarre tastes defy classification.

'Picture the scene, Pamplemousse. It is night in a strange country. This poor, defenceless woman, knowing not a single word of the language, decides to take a stroll in the woods, her two infants suckling at her breasts. Suddenly, when she reaches the darkest part of the forest, she is pounced upon by a pervert. A pervert, Pamplemousse, who not content with waylaying her, begins to gloat over the innocent, down-covered heads of her charges, pawing at them like an *homme* possessed. It is scarcely credible the lengths to which some people will go in order to assuage their base desires.'

'Was she able to provide a description of this man, *Monsieur*?'

'No, Pamplemousse. It was a very dark part of the woods.' The director gazed at him. 'But it seems there was a dog involved. A very large dog.'

Monsieur Pamplemousse returned the gaze unblinkingly. Pommes Frites did likewise. 'Perhaps, *Monsieur*, it was a case of mistaken identity. As you so wisely said earlier, sometimes things get blown up out of all proportion.'

The sun was shining as he came out of the offices of *Le Guide*. There was, nevertheless, more than a hint of autumn in the air. Pommes Frites paused to leave his mark on a tree. He was obviously back to his old self. More Muscadet than Château d'Yquem.

Monsieur Pamplemousse stopped to call in at a *charcuterie*. It was good to be back again on his own territory. As with Holmes at the end of *The Hound of the Baskervilles*, he was about to turn his thoughts into more pleasant channels. He ordered a selection of cold meats for lunch; a *saucisson* or two for the first course. Doucette was preparing a *blanquette de veau*. Then it would be Jean-Claude's turn. Afterwards, if the others went out, he might show him his record collection.

A little further along the rue de Babylone he called in at a *fleuriste* and bought a bouquet of freesias for the girl, suddenly realising as he did so that he didn't even know her name. In his mind she would be for ever Diana. He bought another small bunch for Fräulein Brünnhilde and a bunch of red roses for Doucette; it would establish demarcation lines.

Pommes Frites waited outside the shop for a while and then ran on ahead and waited by the car. He, too, was pleased to be back home. It signalled a return to normality, to walks at set times and his own basket at night. Given a day or two to settle down, his master might even stop calling him Watson.

## ABOUT THE AUTHOR

MICHAEL BOND decided that he wanted to become a writer while serving in the Second World War in the Army, and his first story, written in Egypt about a Cairo nightclub, was written to relieve the boredom of living in a tent. To his surprise, the story was accepted by a London magazine. In 1947 he returned to the BBC, where he had worked during the war, and spent many happy years there as a cameraman. During this time he never stopped writing—short stories, articles, radio and television plays. Among his creations is the beloved series of children's books featuring that charming creature, Paddington Bear. A household name, Paddington Bear has been translated into more than twenty languages. MONSIEUR PAMPLEMOUSSE ON THE SPOT is the third book in Michael Bond's first series of adult novels. Bond lives in London, England.